Sun Chara, a multi-published, JABBIC winner for *Manhattan Millionaire's Cinderella*, writes sexy, hip 'n fun contemporary romance, high adventure historical romance, and any genre that knocks at her imagination. Globetrotting for lore while keeping tabs on Hollywood leads, she loves the challenge of creating stories for book and screen. Designer frappuccinos with whipping cream and sprinkles on top make everyday a celebration!

facebook.com/suncharaauthorpage
@sunchara3

Sun CHARA

Recluse Millionaire, Reluctant Bride

Reluctant Bride

A division of HarperCollins*Publishers*
www.harpercollins.co.uk

Harper*Impulse* an imprint of
HarperCollins*Publishers*
1 London Bridge Street
London SE1 9GF

www.harpercollins.co.uk

A Paperback Original 2018

First published in Great Britain in ebook format
by Harper*Impulse* 2017

Copyright © Sun Chara 2017

Sun Chara asserts the moral right to
be identified as the author of this work

A catalogue record for this book
is available from the British Library

ISBN: 9780008145071

Thank you! To Sensei Joe and Sensei Harry for sharing their wisdom and expertise in the Martial Arts and inspiring unlimited numbers of karatekas!
You are champions!
And most especially, with love to momma for holding down the fort, for being there for me, the Senseis, the karatekas, and everyone! Thank you!
Sweet momma, you are timeless!

Chapter 1

Friday 4:00 a.m.

Stan Rogers had to bring her here, even if he had to resort to 'unusual' methods. He had to get the exotic beauty to agree to his terms. He rubbed the sting from his eyes and the crick from his neck.

A gust of air hurled through the half-open window of his office, bringing with it the scent of Douglas fir. He didn't even flinch at the icy bite on his face. A wake-up call? Rolling up his sleeves, he dismissed the foolish notion and flicked the desk lamp on. The glare sliced across the shadowed room.

He had no choice. It was either her or his son. He'd asked once and she'd refused. Clamping down on the pricking of his conscience, he swiveled in his chair and paced the two burly men's approach.

"Bring her." He slapped his hand on the mahogany desk, his words chips of ice. "Today."

* * *

1

Friday 10:00 a.m.

He was behind it. Stella sensed it in her gut, and that made him a dangerous adversary. Perspiration seeped from her pores and made her jogging suit stick to her skin. A moist drop slid between her breasts. The sun's glare made her squint. Her mind catapulted.

"I asked you to bring her here," he muttered, his words directed at her two sheepish escorts. "But not floundering in a fish net." He bounded over the two steps of the mountain lodge and landed with ease, the gravel crunching beneath his boots.

In two strides, he bridged the distance and halted not two feet from her. His heat filtered to her ... his aftershave ... she wrinkled her nose. Scents of spruce blended with it, and she couldn't place it. Couldn't place him. A niggle nudged her brain, and then vaporized.

"You all right?" he murmured, his hawk-like gaze on her.

Stella's knees almost buckled, and she gripped the trunk of a nearby pine. Her knuckles grazed the bark. A sliver pierced her skin, and she sucked in a breath, gritting her teeth against the sting of the abrasion.

"Take it off her at once."

While the two bumblers fumbled to extricate her from the twine, Stella staked out her surroundings and zoned in on her captor.

He towered above her, with his legs slightly apart,

and shoved his hands in the back pockets of his jeans; the movement stretched his sweater—of Native Indian design—taut across his chest, hinting at the muscle beneath. His casual stance bespoke of power, ownership, confidence.

Sexual energy.

Her side stitched a warning.

He looked rugged as the Canadian Rockies, and hard. Flint hard.

Autumn sunlight glinted off the gold in his hair. A shade lighter than his close-cropped beard, it brushed his shoulders. His laser-sharp eyes reminded her of an ocean storm ... dark, turbulent. The oddest feeling rocked her stomach; the force of his gaze set off signals of another sort in her brain, yet unclear. Through the racket in her head, a spark of a memory flared, but she couldn't grasp it.

"This is the ogre," she murmured to herself. Goosebumps skittered on her skin, and not entirely caused by the November air piercing her clothes.

The flick, *Shrek*, flashed through her mind, and a smile struggled for a place on her mouth. She bit it away. The man looming over her didn't appear as a benevolent green giant.

And she was no princess; just an ordinary working girl.

So what did he want with her?

"What's going on?" Stella rubbed her uninjured hand over her arm to ward off the chill. "Explain."

"Of course." He stroked his chin and tilted his head. A golden earring glittered, and it was like a sledge-hammer hit her brain.

Blood drained from her face and her heart smashed against her ribs.

By sheer force of will, she stood her ground and flexed her fingers. At the slightest provocation, her hands could morph to hammer fists. This man, Stan Rogers, could destroy her. She reeled and the past rushed in...

She had stood at the entrance of the downtown high-rise, every nerve in her body on alert, her mind pounding, *this is your last chance*. Hoping the spring rain didn't frizz her hair, she wiggled her foot and the piece of cardboard covering the hole on the bottom of her shoe bumped her big toe. She tapped her toe on the pavement for a better "fit". Dressed in her one and only suit, she'd pinned her hair at the nape of her neck and clipped gold–ninety-nine-cents-worth hoop earrings on her ears. She mustn't look as "hungry" as she felt.

She'd done every menial job on the face of the planet– from dishwasher, to cook, to janitor, to waitress, to sales—to put herself through the University of British Columbia. Her parents back in Toronto had enough to worry about with her two brothers; she didn't want to be an added burden.

Penny-pinching, she managed to scrape enough for a down payment to open her own martial arts studio. But without a solid credit rating, reserve funds and income details, she was considered a high-risk commodity. She laughed but it came out as a groan. Every bank had turned her down.

R&R Financial had built its multi-million-dollar global chain by picking up the high riskers nobody wanted. Stella took a deep breath and let it seep out through her lips, the sound almost a snort. There'd be a catch.

She glimpsed her reflection in the dusky glass and clutched her purse, doubts bombarding her brain. Gulping down her uncertainty, she ventured through the revolving doors into the enemy's lair.

"Give me one good reason why I should spend my hard-earned money on you." Stan Rogers had curled his lip, studying her beneath his shuttered gaze.

"A good businessman would take a risk," she countered, her words brave, but her hands clammy.

"A calculated one." He brushed his fist across his jaw and reclined in his chair, his eyes piercing ... cold. "He'd be a fool to rush in blindly."

He raised his arms and locked his hands behind his neck, flattening the golden hair at his nape. An earring glinted. The muscles of his forearms flexed beneath his rolled-up sleeves, and his shirt with a red tie loose at the open collar, stretched tight across his torso.

"Which are you, Miss ... or should I say Ms. Ryan? A sure thing or a hidden hazard?"

Stella ignored the knock to the preface of her name and edged forward in her chair. "Neither." She met his gaze head on and glimpsed the navy flecks in his irises.

A jolt shot through her.

He laughed, a humorless sound.

She scooted back.

"In my experience, a female is the biggest risk tempting mankind." He unclasped his hands from behind his neck and brought them to rest on the polished surface of the desk. From the blotter, he picked up a pen and twirling it between his fingers, assessed her. "And you're very much a woman."

She barely heard the murmur from his lips, her gaze glued on the pen he toyed with ... *was he imagining it was her?* She laughed, hiding her nervousness. Silly. The door was two feet behind her—a quick exit.

She went on the offensive. "And a male is—" she began, about to string a line of choice words after that particular species but he beat her to it.

"Trustworthy, dependable, steadfast." A grin twitched the corner of his mouth.

"Matter of opinion."

"Dare one ask yours?" he asked.

"Arrogant, self-centered, controlling ..."

He held up a hand. "Present company excepted, of course."

"I wouldn't know."

"I see." He replaced the ballpoint pen on its stand. "Are you an exception to the superficiality of most women?"

"One way to find out."

"And that is?"

"Approve my loan."

Surprise flickered in his eyes but it quickly diminished beneath his frown. He remained silent for so long, she thought she had lost the gamble. Sighing, she stood up to go, but his next words stopped her.

"Done." He hauled himself from the chair. "With a three point higher interest rate. If you default on payment", he paused and delivered his final shot, "I'll clean you out, lock, stock and caboose."

"You bast—"

He arched an eyebrow.

"You've been baiting me."

"Those are the terms." He stepped around, hitched up his pant leg and propped his hip on the edge of the desk. "Take it or leave it."

Stella warred with common sense, with bravado, and with something more ... her determination to build a business for herself. If she accepted his offer, she'd be shackled to him until she paid off the mortgage. It could take years. If she didn't, she'd be "clocking in" at a low wage for someone else to reap the profits. Either way, it would be a grueling cycle.

"Agreed." If she had to slave away at work, she preferred to do it on her own turf.

She extended her hand and he clasped her fingers in a firm grip, the calluses on the ridge of his palm grazing her flesh.

High voltage charged into her. Her heart leapt, her breathing bumpy.

"Sealed," he said, his gaze unwavering.

She snatched her hand away, but it was too late. The scent of his cologne wrapped around her like a forbidden caress, and made her pulse climb. She gulped, feeling like she'd sold herself to him...

That had been four years ago, and she'd never seen the American financier again. He passed her account to one of his associates at the Canadian branch and flown to his New York headquarters. She smirked. On his private jet no doubt. Being a small fry in a pond of sharks, she couldn't turn him a fast profit, and he'd ditched her.

That had left her wondering why he approved her unsecured loan in the first place. Was she about to find out?

Stella shivered.

"Come in, Miss Ryan," Stan invited, studying her.

"We'll talk over lunch."

The Budweiser Lite curls brushing her face but not hiding the smudges on her cheeks were inherited from her Nordic father. Her almond-shaped eyes from her Japanese mother. He knew. He'd Googled her profile. At his blatant scrutiny, her violet-blue pupils glittered with anger.

She was east and west ... light and dark ... fire and ice.

The contrast was striking. Rare.

An exotic beauty—a dangerous beauty.

She made him feel again. Something he didn't want.

A slight tilt of her chin, and she set her mouth in a straight line.

He caught the hint of a quiver on her bottom lip, and his conscience pummeled the vicinity of his heart. His gut turned to lead, his jaw to steel. She had left him no alternative; he had to bring her here.

"What if I don't?" She challenged, taking several steps backward.

"We'll park beneath that pine and rap." Stan stood his ground.

Slender, she moved with the agility and light step of her profession—just as he remembered from their one meeting long ago. At that time, he'd locked her into a contract with a severe penalty clause, for business.

Now, he had to do the same, this time for personal

gain.

At twenty-seven, she gave the impression of a delicate blonde. He curved his mouth but didn't quite make it to a grin. He knew better. The lady had a quiet strength and a determination that couldn't be beaten. Wasn't that what had turned his hand to approve her loan? It had been foolish, of course. But her courage had stirred something inside him—hadn't he fought the same financial battle twenty years ago when he was first stepping out—

Savagely, he hurled the reminder from his mind and trekked to the house. That was then, this was now. He couldn't afford going soft on her.

Not with what was at stake. He had to crack through her defenses and he'd use any means at his disposal.

"Take her to Minni." He tossed the command at the two men bungling to fold the net. A pause on the veranda, and he turned to her. "She'll remove the splinter from your hand."

"I don't need—" she mouthed back, but he disappeared indoors.

Stella dismissed the tick to her pride and raised her arms, stretching.

"Ahh, freedom."

She could ensue another battle, but weary from the first ordeal at the beach and the long bumpy ride, decided to bide her time. An opportunity would present itself. When it did, she'd be ready. In the meantime, sweaty and disheveled, she'd welcome a chance to freshen up before facing him again. Without a doubt, they were headed for another clash.

Joe, the dark-haired body guard escorted her inside the lodge, then left to go find Minni. Fred-the-red stuck to her like glue.

She caught his reflection in the wall mirror; he was shifting on his feet. She grinned. One on one ... better odds. Her hands itched for action, but she wouldn't get far if she made a move now. She scanned the hallway. A Tiffany lamp—a possible weapon—was set on a shelf beneath the mirror.

The coat rack in the corner—another possibility. Beyond the arch in front of her, a stairway curved to the second floor, fueling her curiosity.

"Over there is the living room and library." A petite woman with a motherly smile and warm brown eyes walked through the portal, and Fred backtracked out of sight.

"Opposite on the left is the kitchen," she said in her bubbly voice. "My favorite place." She hugged a first-aid kit to her bosom and motioned for Stella to follow. "By the way, I'm Minni, Joe's wife. I'll be lookin' after ye while ye're here."

"I won't be staying."

"Joe and I've been with Mr. Rogers eight years now,"

Minni rambled on as if she hadn't spoken. "Shoulda heard the goings on 'round here a few months ago. The place turned upside down and all because of that poor child ..." She paused for breath and picked her way up the stairs.

Halfway down the corridor, Minni opened a door and ushered her inside. "Mr. Rogers had this room specially prepared for you."

"He did, did he?" Stella muttered, an uncanny sensation pricking the back of her neck.

"I did."

She spun around. "Too bad you wasted your time."

"Time is money, Ms. Ryan." Stan winked at Minni. "I never waste either one." He walked right past her, ruffling air between them. A hint of his scent floated to her. Fresh as the outdoors, it should have soothed, but instead, it made her ire rise.

"Nor do I," she fired back, but he'd already bounded down the stairs.

"Come on then," Minni called from inside the room.

Stella debated, thinking the ogre took a lot for granted, but the best she could do now was get as much information as she could. Smiling, she stepped through the door ... and Minnie was her source.

"So, this a busy place?"

"It can be." Minnie plonked the first-aid kit on a stack of magazines on the bureau by the bed, bumping the long-stemmed red rose in the crystal vase. "This won't hurt a bit."

Stella extended her hand. "You like living up here?" She scoped the room. Sunlight filtered through the curtains of a window—a possible escape route—she filed that away in her mind. "Ouch!" She winced as Minnie yanked out the splinter with a pair of tweezers.

"There, that should do it." She smiled and blotted the scratches with antiseptic.

Stella turned to thank her and a splash of solid color on the bed caught her eye. She stretched across the laced bedspread and shoving the cushions aside, snatched up the uniform—a Karate gui.

"Hope it fits." Minni fussed around her with a Band-Aid in her hand.

"Why?"

Minni turned quiet. After she bandaged her knuckles, she patted her hand. "There." She swept up the first-aid kit and murmuring about lunch, made her exit.

Stella made a beeline for the window, turned the latch and raised it. She leaned out and gauged the distance to the ground. Too high to jump but she could climb down. Just then, Fred-the-red appeared from behind the corner of the house and gave her a brief nod. She waved a half-hearted greeting, realizing she'd have to be extra quiet and time it just right.

On her way to the bathroom, she paused to smell

the rose and sucked in a breath, the force of it burning her throat. Her face was splashed on the cover of the magazine topping the stack on the dresser. Headlining the current issue of *Sports Unlimited*, Stella Ryan: the woman, the sensei, and the competitor at the International Karate Tournament in Tokyo. Air pressure fizzed between her teeth. She bolted into the bathroom and locked the door.

Twisting on the shower, she stepped beneath, the warm spray soothing her body, but not her mind. Two minutes tops, and she swabbed herself dry. Throwing on her clothes, she wondered what other surprises ... er ... shocks were in store for her.

Preferring to face-off her demons, Stella marched downstairs and halted outside the dining room. She wiped her damp palms on her thighs, took a deep breath to steady her nerves and pushed the double panels open. She paused on the threshold.

Eight chairs fringed a table in the centre of the floor, the lace table cloth and sparkling crystal were a marked contrast to the somber tones of the room. Minnie's feminine touch, she thought, not missing that this was to be a lunch *á deux*...

"Come in, Ms. Ryan."

The ogre's gruff voice made her jump, and she hesitated for a fraction of a second. She'd always confronted that which she feared and thereby conquered it. This

... this man would be no exception. She took a bold step inside and another until she stood in the middle of the room.

He stood behind the bar, choking a bottleneck between his fingers, his intense gaze shooting into her. She cringed at her choice of words and her bandaged hand flew to her throat. Chills chased up her spine. She stood her ground and glared back at him.

Silence fueled the room. Thickened. Smothered.

He feigned a cough and splashed Scotch into a glass. The sound of liquid over ice shattered the tension between them. Stella dropped her hand to her side. She was trained to protect herself, her body her weapon ... *yeah, but here you are anyway.*

"What's your pleasure?" He seized the tumbler and motioned to an army of liqueurs on the counter. In a lazy sweep, his eyes toured her head to toe, then his lashes flickered, concealing a glint of something indefinable in his pupils.

A blush warmed her skin.

"My pleasure is to get out of here," she snapped on an intake of breath. Boldly, she allowed her eyes to do some appraising of their own.

Fortyish. Over six-feet. He exuded strength and power.

Raw sexuality.

Her stomach flipped. Her heart raced.

The walls seemed to close in.

She shook her head, blinked. This man could crush her. She inhaled a mouthful of oxygen. Exhaled. *Okay*. She twitched her lips, but didn't smile. She knew from experience that size and strength were not the key. The right move combined with speed and accuracy could bring anyone down. Including Stan Rogers.

Tempting.

But, timing played into it and this was not quite the moment for it. Patience was not her greatest virtue.

"I figured you'd prefer clean clothes after your shower." Stan took a swig of the amber liquid and studied her over the rim, amusement tugging the corner of his mouth.

"You figured wrong." She ventured forward a few paces, not wanting him to think she was afraid. "I'll wear what I please, when I please and how I please. And, I'm not in the habit of wearing borrowed threads and certainly" –she paused for effect— "I don't dine in a Karate gui."

"Of course." He brushed a thumb across his fuzzy chin. "A sweaty jogging suit is so" –his gaze dropped several notches, zeroing in on the rise and fall of her breasts— "much more appealing."

Stella was about to blast him with a string of verbal bullets, when he held up a hand, warding off her attack.

"How remiss of me not to consider your lack of

attire," he said, a tone of formality in his voice.

Stella twisted her lips. *Attire? Get with the times, mister.*

"I'll speak to Minni about it."

"Don't bother." She narrowed her eyes, sizing him up like an opponent in a ring. "I intend to leave here within the hour, and if you try to stop me, I'll have you charged with kidnapping."

"You're not a prisoner here, Ms. Ryan," he said, tone cool. "You're an invited guest with whom I wish to discuss business."

"Why didn't you call or e-mail or drop by my studio to discuss your ... er ... business?"

"In a sense, I did."

"Stop talking in riddles."

He shrugged.

And that had her hackles rising.

"This charade is utter nonsense." She moved another few steps closer, the table a barrier between them. "I don't like being manhandled."

The deep sound of his laughter ricocheted off the walls. "Heard it was the other way around." He saluted her with his drink.

Stella shook her head, pointing her finger at him. "Look here, I have a business to run. Right now, my students are at the dojo waiting for me."

Stan set the empty glass on the gleaming countertop

and rubbed his palms together. "Took care of it."

"I demand to be relea—" She gaped at him. "What does that mean?" she demanded. "You know you could be arrested."

"My men—"

"Thugs."

"—left a memo at your studio explaining your absence."

"Disappearance."

He shuttered his eyes to blue slits, considering her veiled warning. "Ms. Ryan, I'm offering you my hospitality as my guest."

"I'm not your guest." She tossed her head. "And don't need or want anything from you."

He hiked a brow, and she swallowed a lump in her throat. Of course, he had control of her core asset and—

"You're on a publicity tour ... Tokyo, Toronto ... family demands," he explained, his words saturated with meaning. "You'd be returning soon."

"You dared to—" A tremor vibrated from her head to her toes, shivers prancing on her spine.

He shrugged. "A risk worth taking."

Stella paled, their one and only meeting zooming to the forefront of her mind.

"Something wrong, Ms. Ryan?" Casually, he slid his hands in his pockets, confident he'd cornered her.

Stella groped for the back of a chair, the wood smooth

and hard beneath her fingertips.

Like the man—unbreakable.

"Do you often take such risks?" she tested, her voice brittle.

"Occasion—"

"Why?"

"High stakes."

"How lofty are they this time?" She tightened her grip on the chair, her heart pounding a warning.

"Riskiest bet of my life," he admitted.

She wouldn't be bridled. "Must be, to ditch your life of the rich and famous for that of a recluse."

He laughed, a dark, ominous sound. "It is." A shadow swept across his eyes, and a nerve pinched his jaw. He shrugged and didn't elaborate.

Tenderness pierced through her frustration. She must be mistaken, or nuts. Nuts to feel anything but contempt for the ogre. She shoved the pinch of feeling away. She didn't care, couldn't care, refused to care.

"I don't play cat and mouse games, Mr. R."

"You do remember."

The gray at his temples and his beard had thrown her at first. His electrifying blue eyes and commanding tone, capped off with his baiting remarks, cued her a second time in as many hours, how well he knew the game of finance and how well he wielded the rules for his benefit. Yes, she remembered him. He was not a man she could easily forget, nor could she forget how ruthless he could be.

"How do I fit into your scheme of things this time?" Stella asked, her voice crackling with ice.

"Predominantly."

Chapter 2

Stella's gaze clashed with his, taut emotion vibrating between them.

Seconds ticked by, seeming endless.

Minni walked in with their lunch and the tension in the air snapped.

"Come, you'll feel better after you've eaten." Stan stepped to the table and pulled out a chair for her.

Stella didn't move.

"Hope you're hungry, dear," Minni said, her mouth tilting at the corners. "I've cooked my favorite Italian recipe with a Scottish zing." She giggled and her hand fluttered to her mouth.

"It smells delicious." Stella eyed the hot rolls, the salad, the sticky chocolate cake that was for dessert.

Stan draped an arm around his housekeeper's shoulders and winked. "Minni is the best cook in town and I've got her."

Stella's pulse faltered. He wanted, he got. Well, he

hadn't gotten her.

She should feel more joy ... maybe it was because she was hungry.

Minni blushed. "Oh, get on with you." She smoothed an imaginary crease on her apron and pushed the trolley from the room.

Another uncomfortable silence ensued ... delectable aroma of lasagna, crowned with bubbly cheese wafted to her and her stomach growled. Stella plunked down on the chair across from the enemy, hoping he hadn't heard.

He took his own seat and began serving.

"You should try some," he said between mouthfuls. "It's good."

She hesitated, her mouth mutinous, her taste buds watering. Finally ... "I'll have a little."

A smart man, he said nothing, simply grunted his approval.

Not that she needed *his* approval about anything, but she was ravenous ... no use letting good food go to waste.

At last, she placed the remaining piece of cake in her mouth and stole a glance at him from beneath her eyelashes. Why was he grinning? She licked her lips. His grin disappeared, his gaze darkening. Thinking, chocolate smudged her chin, she swiped at it with her finger and licked the tip. A sound from deep in his throat ... a low growl?

"Something amusing?" she snapped, a flush warming her cheeks.

"You look like a sixteen-year old stuffing that cake in your mouth." His lips twitched in wry amusement.

"Good thing I'm not, or you'd be compounding the charge of kidnapping with that of a minor."

He squashed the grin between his lips, his cheekbones prominent, a storm brewing in his eyes. "I won't dignify that with a response."

Her emotions were bopping, and she wanted to let fly at him, but thought better of it. *Control.* She could match him in that couldn't she?

"More coffee?" He picked up the coffee pot and waited.

At her nod, his mouth cracked a fraction, and he filled her cup to the brim. Rich flavor steamed the air. She cradled the cup between her palms and watched him pour another cup for himself.

His lips curved over straight white teeth, and his lower lip a bit fuller gave his mouth an added sensuality. She could just imagine him nibbling ... She lowered her eyes to his hands. The man seized whatever he wanted. A shiver shot through her ... whomever he desired. Yet, she couldn't turn away. His sleeves were pushed up almost to his elbows, golden hair feathered his forearms, his muscles defined even by the simple task of pouring coffee.

Slamming the brakes on her thoughts, she tipped the cup to her lips.

"Easy, it's hot," Stan warned.

Too late, Stella felt the unwelcome singe on her tongue. "I know now, it's hot," she sputtered, dropping the cup back, liquid splashing into the saucer. Grabbing the glass of water beside her plate, she gulped a mouthful and soothed her stinging tongue.

"Good thing that." A hint of a smile lingered on his lips, and his gaze strayed to the curve of her breast, barely visible by the tear in her sweatshirt.

His eyes darkened, shuttered, his smile vanished.

Her eyes grew wide, lashes fluttering, shielding.

Signals ... danger ... combustion.

Stella took another gulp of water. "I-it's not funny."

"Never said it was."

"The burn stung."

"I know."

Heat infused her body. Was there a double-entendre in that? She set the glass on the table with more force than necessary; the liquid swirled against the clear walls, but didn't spill. Too bad. She felt like doing injury to something or, she glanced at the man beside her, someone. He certainly didn't think she could be contained against her will without retaliating?

Tossing a crumpled napkin on the table, he pushed his chair back and motioned her to the sofa by the window. For a second, she debated whether to sit or stand, but not wanting him to think she was on the defensive, plopped on the settee. He lounged on the armchair across from her, trapping her in the lens of his vision like a high-powered combatant's target.

Breath pocketed in her chest, and she pushed up her sleeves, on guard.

"Stella, I, or rather we" –he crossed one leg over his knee— "have followed your career as a martial artist for some time. Rare to see a woman master the art of self-defense to the professionalism you've achieved."

"Thank you," she said, wondering where this was leading. If he thought he could lull her into a false security with compliments to get what he wanted from her, he was wrong.

Dead wrong.

"This woman was worth the risk, after all." She couldn't help the jab.

"Financially, yes," he hit back, his tone all business. "You've proved a worthwhile asset."

A silent growl built in Stella's throat. How dared he talk like she was some inanimate object. Asset, indeed. "So, why bring me here?"

"I wanted the very best for Troy. No one else would do," he murmured more to himself than to her.

"You wanted the very best of what?" she asked, her curiosity pushing anger aside. "Who's Troy? And what does he have to do with me?"

A silent moment passed, and he leaned forward, his midnight blue eyes boring into her. "I want to hire you as my son's martial arts coach."

"Troy."

"That's right."

"This is ludicrous. Absolutely wild." She nearly burst out laughing but some innate sense checked it in her throat. "There are plenty of martial arts schools you could enroll him in. There was no need for you and your ... er ... friends to go through this farce to bring me here. Even if you wanted me as his Sensei—"

"Instructor."

She nodded. "I'd have been happy to coach him at my studio."

"I didn't want Troy in a public class, stared at, ridiculed by other children." He brushed a hand across his chin. "My son needs a private coach." His voice deepened, hinting at a deeper, conflicting emotion. "You, Ms. Ryan, will teach him until he feels confident ... strong again."

Children could be cruel, but for him to take these extreme measures to get her here was beyond her comprehension. "I don't understand."

He paused for a moment, the silence deafening. "He must become healthy again. Feel like a valued human being."

Was he playing on her emotions? Could he have an ulterior motive?

"I'm sorry, Mr. Rogers," she said, recalling how callous he could be. "I have a full schedule." Ignoring her erratic pulse, she cleared her throat and scooted forward. "I've spent years building my business and Karate is my life." She'd practically starved to do it, but he didn't have to know that. "I can't abandon it for the whim of a father and his son." Her words sounded abrasive even to her own ears, but she had to be tough.

Tough with him.

And tougher with herself, because the man was dangerous to her heart, her emotions, her mind ... to her whole self.

In one fluid motion, Stan hauled himself from the armchair, eyes blazing and nostrils flaring. Startled, Stella squared her shoulders and shuttered her gaze, ready to dodge if necessary.

"What do you know of pain? Of a child tossed about like chattel who's—" He shoved a hand through his hair and paced the room, his outburst surprising him more than it did her. "I apologize. You're not to blame." His jaw clenched. "Trauma, especially recurring, can scar for life."

Stella uttered not a word.

Dangerous didn't describe him. Lethal was more accurate.

The man was lethal.

"When a child is involved, one can become ballistic."

"And are you?"

"What?" He glanced at her, a blank look across his features.

"Ballistic?"

An unwilling smile flittered across his mouth but he neither confirmed nor denied.

Her pulse leaped. His demeanor oozed sexual energy. Moisture glazed her upper lid. She swabbed it with her thumb, and his eyes zoomed in on her mouth.

A silent moment, a tense moment, a telling moment.

She didn't want to know ... acknowledge the shift in the atmosphere between them. She had to be smart, strong, deliver her blow and get out of there. Fast.

So, she said the only thing that came to her mind, "What's the matter with him? Your son?"

"That's not your concern." His words were like ice chaffing her skin.

"All right," she said. "Why don't you teach him how to fight." She scrutinized the length and breadth of his body to the detriment of another leaping heartbeat. "You ... uh ... look capable."

"I could teach him to use his fists, but street fighting isn't the best for him." He caught and held her in his sights, a wry twist on his mouth.

Stella struggled, yet didn't move an inch. But her vitals

were going haywire. She had to get out of here, get out ... get some air.

"Martial arts, the ancient art of self-defense, exercising the spirit, mind and body would suit him better," he insisted.

A time bomb was ticking.

"Take the job."

"No!" She leaped to her feet.

"No?"

She mocked a cough to hide her discomfort, and reverted to her business persona. "I'd like to help, but it's out of the question."

"Think again," he said, voice smooth, silky. "Do it for three months."

"I couldn't teach your son Karate in that time," she said, voice soft. *Was she weakening? Where was her tough stance?* "It's a lifetime thing."

"I understand." In two strides, he bridged the gap between them, crowding her. "But it would give him a start. Some basics."

"True."

He was so close, his body heat warmed, his breath fanned her cheek, the faint scent of Scotch making her want to taste ... him. She folded her hands into fists, determined to chase away this overwhelming rush that had her heart battering her chest.

"A philosophy, a discipline underscores the Martial

Arts." She forced the words out. "More important is when and how to use defense technique."

"I know," Stan said. "That's why I didn't want to hire just anyone."

"You're flattering me, Mr. Rogers," Stella said, lowering her lashes a fraction. "However, three months is impossible." Good, when she didn't look at him, she sounded herself, the savvy businesswoman. "I've scheduled events I can't get out—"

"Can't or won't."

"You'll find someone else to help your boy." She dared lift her lashes ... a mistake. Her breath swept out of her, leaving her deflated. "Someone willing to be on call ..." She was fighting herself more than him.

His gaze turned steely. "As you could find another to refinance your mortgage next term."

He'd beat her to it, delivering his blow first. A hit to the gut.

"You're playing dirty."

"I have no choice."

"I'd have no problem renewing my mortgage from another investment firm," she tested, every muscle in her body contracting. "Financially, I'm a worthy asset, remember."

He laughed, the harsh sound grating in the tense atmosphere between them. "A solid investment would be considered." He curled his mouth into a cruel smile.

"With so many foreclosures in this business, very few would bite anything else. Too risky."

"I have good credit," she blurted, a slight waver in her voice.

"Sure now?"

Stella shoved him back, another blunder; touching him rocked her to her toes. He didn't move, so she did. Back two steps, three ... a raging flame ignited her words. "You wouldn't dare mess with my credentials."

His jaw jutted, and the flecks of navy in his eyes turned granite. "We'll have you, Ryan, or no one." His veiled threat hung in the air.

She glared at him long and hard. Oxygen fueled her lungs and shot out of her. She'd never run from anyone in her life and she didn't intend to start now. "What you want" —she advanced two steps closer to reclaim her space— "you get, by fair means or foul" —another step brought her within an inch of him— "is that it?"

"You have a problem with that?" He bent his head within an inch of her mouth, his breath a caress.

She would not start hyperventilating. She would not. Steeling her nerves, she gave him stare for stare. Dear God, she was falling into the ocean of his eyes.

He shifted.

Relief. Breathing room.

Or was that an illusion. Was he preparing for another hit?

Doubts zigzagged through her mind; her temples throbbed. She had learned never to allow an opponent to sense her uncertainty and here she was, letting him shake her confidence. Quickly regrouping, she stiffened her spine and raised her chin. She wouldn't wait to see what he would do. She'd go on the offensive, deliver her strike and get out of the ring.

"I'm sorry you went to all the trouble to get me here, but I must decline your offer of employment." She prayed her refusal sounded intractable this time. Without the renewal of her mortgage on terms she could afford, she could lose her business, her livelihood, her future. A quiver tore through her, but she stood resolute.

"Stubborn woman," he muttered beneath his breath. "Haven't learned to cut your losses yet, have you, Ryan?"

"I don't intend to have any."

"Don't push my hand," he growled, stalking to the window and contemplating the outdoors.

Stella stared daggers at his rigid back.

Finally he turned, his gaze frosty. "Fred will drive you back to town."

She started in surprise. "You're letting me go?"

"Isn't that what you wanted?" he queried.

Chapter 3

"Yes."

He searched her face, then nodded in acquiescence.

Unusual. Him being so accommodating.

Stella rubbed her nape, settling fine hair on end. Until she was safely tucked in her own bed, she wouldn't put anything past him.

"The library's down the hall ... you can wait there." He strode to the door, tossing over his shoulder, "When it's time, Minni will come for you."

"Thank you," Stella murmured, surprised she'd uttered the civil words. But by then, she stood alone in the middle of the dining room, so he must've missed them. For some inexplicable reason, she felt deserted.

Foolish, girl.

She strolled to the library and her shoulders sagged. No computer, no cell phone. Just shelves of books, comfy furniture and flames blazing in the grate. Cozy.

Warm. Unlike the owner. Either he enjoyed his solitude or turned into a recluse for some reason. His son?

Browsing, she pulled out a volume, by-passed the sofa and sat cross-legged on the carpet. Logs crackled and hissed, shooting off sparks. Absent-mindedly, she flipped the pages, her mind wandering to her captor. It was obvious he loved his son, but a harshness under-lined it, sharp and cutting in intensity. Who or what had caused the bitterness in his life? And how much did it have to do with him taking such drastic measures to bring her here, then quickly releasing her? Hmm, she set her mind on rewind...

Stella had been jogging along the English Bay beach walk near her studio home as dawn colored the sky when the two men accosted her.

"We're not here to hurt you, Miss," the man said, dressed in a dark suit and smoothing his reddish mustache.

"That's right." The other one flipped his dark hair off his brow with the back of his hand, revealing a mole at his temple.

The simple action triggered her memory.

"You two came to my studio last week," Stella said, gauging them.

"That's right," the red-haired one admitted. "Since you turned his offer down, we ... er ... are inviting you to come see the boss himself."

"Yeah, that's right," the dark one agreed. "We're to drive you there."

"You tell boss-man," Stella bit out, "if he wants to talk to me, he can telephone and make an appointment at a decent hour at the studio."

"It isn't that simple, Miss," the man in front of her answered. "He—"

"Listen, I have a business to run," she cut him off, starting to backtrack away from them. "If you don't mind, I'd like to get back to it."

The two men glanced at one another. "We hoped it wouldn't come to this." One sighed, the other shrugged, and both made a grab for her.

She'd fought them, but when they threw the fishing net over her, she was caught...

Stella shifted on the carpet and eased the cramps from her knees. She may be caught, but not for long. Warmth from the fire soothed, and she turned on her side, cushioning her head on her folded arms.

"Mmm, this feels nice," she murmured.

The altercation with his two goons, followed so soon with the confrontation with the ogre, had left her physically and emotionally exhausted.

She lowered her lashes, just for a second.

After what seemed mere moments, Stella fluttered her eyes open, prickles on the back of her neck. Except for the flickering flames in the grate, the room had grown dark, the sun having set long ago. She blinked to orientate herself to her surroundings and collided with his electrifying gaze.

"What're you doing here?" She leaped up and swayed at the sudden movement. Calm as you please, he lounged on the sofa, watching her beneath his bushy brows. Feeling at a distinct disadvantage, she swept up the pillow and blanket from the floor, and hugged them to her bosom.

Stan had the urge to snake his arm out and haul her into his arms, burying his face in her hair, sliding his hands beneath her disheveled jogging suit ... sweat and all. He didn't care. Her warmth and her scent, with a hint of the Ivory soap she'd used during her shower, lassoed him.

His gut jerked, or was that his heart?

Her eyes a deep sapphire from slumber, mesmerized. He wanted to nuzzle her nape, taste ... abruptly, he checked the motion.

Utter foolishness.

Hadn't he learned his lesson in college when he got hitched on a dare? She'd taken him for a ride ... every penny he had ... and still after his scalp ... and his son. Then, he'd been young, proud, reckless. Now, older and he hoped wiser— *What the heck are you doing with this woman here?* He shrugged the irksome thought aside.

If he wanted a woman, he could get one at the snap

36

of his fingers. They were easy to come by when one was endowed with wealth. He wondered if they wanted him or his loot—if they'd even glance his way if he pumped gas at the local garage. He curled his lip in a silent snarl, and, thinking it was directed at her, Stella took a step away from him.

Fever.

Blood pulsed through his veins and pooled in his groin. He bit down an expletive. He didn't want a woman, not now. And certainly, not this one. Too stubborn, too shrewd, too outspoken, too beautiful ... he sucked in a breath and let it blast out between his teeth.

"Is it time to go?" she asked.

Let her go? Never again.

"A change of plans," he said, not quite meeting her eyes.

"Oh?" Stella moistened her lips with the tip of her tongue.

Sexual awareness flared. Stan tightened his jaw.

"You won't be leaving today, after all." At her outraged expression, he was quick to add, "A problem with the truck." Under the circumstances, he had trouble believing the lame excuse himself. Just happened to be true s'all. Whether she believed him or not was her problem. *Yeah, right.*

"How convenient."

"Actually, it's not," he muttered. "The group wanted

to get to town and stock supplies before first snow."

"Snow?"

He ignored her query. "Fred was going to check on the limo and halfway there, the Hummer broke down. He had to hike back."

"Poor him."

He didn't even blink at her sarcastic rejoinder. "The outing will be postponed until tomorrow, together with your return." A pause and, "Poor you?"

"Go to he—"

"I've already been," he ground out. "Don't recommend it."

About to shoot back, she thought better of it. Stoking the already volatile situation wouldn't get her out of there. And that's what she wanted.

Definitely.

"Doesn't look like snow to me, not by a long shot," she said again.

"At least not for another couple of months."

"We like to be prepared in case it's early this year." He hauled himself off the sofa and reached out for the blanket and pillow.

She clutched them tighter, like a protective device. "What about trekking to the limo and driving from there?"

"Not in this darkness, unless it's an absolute emergency," he said, tone flat. "Dangerous, especially if you're not familiar with the trail."

"To me, this is an emergency."

"Not enough to risk a broken leg in a pot hole. Be serious, Ms. Ryan." He raised a brow. "What's one more day going to matter? You could leave early tomorrow without risk."

What he said made sense, but she didn't have to like it. She certainly didn't want to stay shacked up with him, miles from anywhere. It was time to be proactive, and get her own ticket outa this sticky mess.

"You're invited for dinner. Minni'll—"

"I'm not hungry."

"Fine."

His indifference infuriated ... then she glanced down at the bedding in her hands. Odd, she hadn't had them when she first lay down by the fireside.

She frowned, and an image pushed its way to the forefront of her mind. Somewhere between sleep and wakefulness, she'd felt a gentle hand lift her head and slip the pillow beneath ... cover her with the blanket. She thought she'd been dreaming but—

"Did ... uh ... you bring the blanket?"

He shrugged. "Didn't want you catching cold."

"Thank—"

"A sick Karate coach wouldn't do me any good," he said, cutting off her polite remark with his callous words.

Jerk. She threw the blanket at him.

He caught it. "Your hand must be okay."

The pillow followed. He ducked and it sailed over his head, landing on the sofa behind him.

"Mad about something, Ryan?" He rubbed his earring with his thumb, his face the picture of innocence. "I was only thinking of your well-being."

"Don't do me any favors, Rogers," she snapped. "And to think that I'd begun—" She skidded to a halt.

"You were saying," he prompted, amusement twitching the corner of his mouth.

"None of your business." She turned her back to him and stared at the fire in the grate.

A few flickers struggled to survive. Overly confined, flames couldn't breathe, fizzled out. She was starting to feel like that and she resented it.

Controlled wildfire could sweep across ... clear ... a new beginning. He'd done that for her four years ago, when he financed her dojo; she would not let him take that away from her.

Pressure seemed to be building around him, and she pitied the person who got caught in its explosive wake. A showing was sure to be in the cards ... and she'd bet, soon. She'd skip out long before then and not get trapped in the crossfire.

Her temples throbbed. She'd almost believed the story about his son. Wha-a-at? She hadn't seen a child around. And the burning question—where was the wife?

"If you change your mind, dinner is at eight. Be prompt." The deep timbre of his voice skewered her thoughts aside, and she glanced over her shoulder to see the door closing behind him. Immediately, his arm shot around the jamb. He flicked on the light switch, withdrew and was gone.

Stella blinked from the sudden glare and sank on the couch. Hugging the pillow, she laid her head upon it—too bad she'd missed her target ... him. He rattled her, stirring feelings inside her that were yet unclear. She wanted to dismiss the emotion together with the man who lit the fuse. She laughed, a humorless sound. That would be impossible. One couldn't disregard a man like Stan Rogers, not with his magnetism, his potent sexuality. Hate him, yes, ignore him, never.

* * *

Stella declined dinner and paced the floor of her room, plotting her course of action. In a few hours, everyone would be asleep. Except her.

In the meantime, she had to contend with hunger pangs pummeling her stomach. Eight hours had passed since lunch, and the mouth-watering aromas drifting upstairs from the kitchen didn't help matters. She leafed through a magazine, realized it was upside down and slapped it back on the stack. She sighed, and flicked on the TV, changed her mind and flicked it off. She had to concentrate ... focus. Her mind veered to the bearded man and a million questions flittered through her mind.

A sudden knock on the door made her jump and she turned, alert.

Minni opened the door and stepped inside, balancing a tray in her hands.

"Oh, Minni, you're a lifesaver." Stella seized the tray laden with food before it toppled to the floor.

"'Twas Mr. Rogers' idea." She winked and smoothed her hands over her apron. "He thought ye might be hungry by now. Said ye could pout all ye want, but eat something ye must."

Stella snatched a cheese sandwich and bit into it with gusto, barely hearing her gentle reprimand. Almost choking on the piece, she forced it down and grabbed the glass of milk.

"Mmm, this is absolutely delicious," she mumbled between mouthfuls, rolling her eyes. "Thanks, Min."

"Not at all, Miss," Minni replied. "'Tis a pleasure to have a fresh young face around here for a change. We don't get many visitors up here."

"I'm not surprised." What with the ogre ordering everyone around. "It's so far away," she added, dabbing her mouth with a napkin.

"Not at all," Minni said. "This being one of the lower peaks of the Coast Range" –she paused and calculated—

"wedged between Grouse and Whistler, it's about an hour from the main road to Vancouver."

Bingo.

Stella drained the glass and set it back on the tray. The hike to the road would take about half an hour. If she managed to make it that far and was lucky to catch a bus on its last run, she'd be snoozing in her own bed by midnight. It was risky, but she was determined to try.

"Minni, do you mind if I ask you something?" Stella reached for an apple and buffed it to a shine across her sleeve. "Where's the boy and his mom?"

"Mrs. Rogers doesn't live here." Minni straightened her apron and fidgeted with the ruffled edges. "As for the boy, he's—"

At that moment, Stan bellowed from below and the woman started, breaking off mid-sentence. Stella could have screamed.

"Goodnight, lass." Minni hurried out, mumbling about grocery lists to discuss before retiring for the night.

Drat the man! Stella bit into the apple, imagining it was a part of his anatomy she dug her teeth into. Juice dribbled down her chin. She flicked it off with her fingers, licked them clean and tasted sweet tartness.

Moments later, Stella set the tray in the hallway and listened.

Whispers of voices filtered up the stairs, and she closed the door. Stepping across to the bed, she bounced on the edge a couple of times and lay down.

Her eyelids felt heavy. She stretched her arms above her head, contemplated the wooden beams of the ceiling and counted backwards from one hundred. By the time she got to one, she closed her eyes. Bliss. The bed was so comfortable and she was so very tired ... she mustn't fall asleep, mustn't...

The sound of a door slamming echoed through the walls and startled her from her semi-doze. She pushed hair off her face, rubbed her eyes and yawned. A pause, and she slid off the bed. It creaked. She froze. When she didn't hear anything, she tiptoed to the door and opened it a crack.

The tray was gone and tranquility filled the lodge. She closed the door, leaned her head on the jamb and counted to ten. Twisting around, she hurried to the window and raised the already half open shutter. Pungent forest scents sailed to her. The night was dark as a witch's cauldron and still as a cat about to pounce. A nervous giggle bounced its way up her throat, and she slammed her hand over her mouth. A moonbeam flitted from behind a cloud, and trees swayed in the breeze, creating ghostly images.

Stella took a deep breath, exhaled, and climbed over the ledge onto the roof. Crouching like a cat burglar, she was ready to jump but changed her mind and crawled forward, peeking over the edge. A drainage pipe swiveled down the side of the building. She grabbed onto it, the metal felt cold and hard beneath her fingers as she inched her way to the ground. Almost there, she missed her footing, swallowed her scream and careened off, landing with a thud. She scrambled to her feet, dusted herself off, thankful that no bones were broken. Bruised, she rubbed her tush.

Night breeze smacked her hot face and pierced through her one layer of clothing, chilling her sweaty skin. She shivered and wrapped her arms about herself. Staring at the trail disappearing into the eerie forest, Stella wondered if she'd made a smart decision.

The tense moment passed, and she chuckled, shaking off the foreboding. Tiptoeing to the garage, she stepped through the half open door and rummaged the shelves for a flashlight. She would return it by mail; she eased her conscience.

Suddenly, lights blazed.

Her heart vaulted into her throat. She raised a hand to shield her eyes from the brightness and someone grabbed her. She screamed.

Chapter 4

"I should've known you'd try something foolhardy."

Stella struggled to pull out of his arms. "Leave me alone, Rogers." She stomped hard on his foot and he loosened his hold a fraction. In that instant she wrenched free, served him a front kick to the abdomen and dashed from the garage.

"Spitfire." He tackled her and she tumbled to the ground, breath knocked out of her. Flipping her on her back, he straddled her and pulled her arms over her head, imprisoning them in his grip. "What now, my Karate gal?"

"You infuriating, no good—"

"Didn't think you'd run from a challenge, Ryan."

Wriggling beneath him, she kicked her legs in the air and twisted her arms to escape him.

"Thought you were tougher." Stan leaned closer and looked deep into her eyes, the bristle of his chin a stimulant on her skin. "Hmm, could I have made a mistake ... rarely known to happen, but with you—"

"You pompous a—"

He yanked her up so fast, she slammed into his chest, breath bursting out of her. Moonlight cast shadows across his features—his eyes, his cheekbones ... his mouth ... him.

Dark. Mysterious. Sensual.

He lowered his head, his lips a feather breadth from her own, his breath a warm caress upon her skin. A puff of air caught in her throat. Beneath her hands, his heart pounded to the wild beat of her own.

"Come on." With his hand firmly on her elbow, he walked her to the house, an impatient rhythm to his stride. "I told you Fred would drive you home tomorrow. Now, go to bed."

"All right, all right." She skirted around him into the hallway, the sting of her words scouring her tongue. Anger was directed more at herself than at him, because what he said made sense.

*　*　*

Stella fluttered her eyelashes open and squinted at the clock on the wall. Six-thirty a.m. In limbo for a second, she yawned and everything rushed back in her mind. She groaned. Throwing off the covers, she slid out of bed and headed to the window. She peered up at the sky. Sunshine filtered through fluffy clouds.

Relief. No snow.

Forest creatures heralded the beginning of a new day, and nature's serenity washed over her. She turned away, lifting the flannel nightgown Minni had left for her the night before, over her head.

A scream pierced the air.

She froze in mid-motion, and the nightie fell back in place over her body. The shrill sound penetrated the walls again. She yanked the door open and flew into the hallway, pausing a second to determine its direction.

Muffled weeping.

Stella hurried to a half-open door several yards away and tiptoed inside. Except for a faint nightlight, the drawn drapes shrouded the room.

She blinked to adjust her eyes to the dimness and saw him. The child lay curled beneath the blankets on the bed, his head half buried under the pillow, his sobs echoing around her. She stepped nearer and brushed his shoulder with a gentle hand.

"Mommy." He hiccupped on a sob and peeked at her from beneath his woolen fortress, his damp lashes fringing his blue eyes.

A hit in the gut. They were the exact replica of the ogre's.

She swiped her moist palms on her nightgown and sat on the edge of the bed; he fell into her arms. Rocking him into a semi-doze, she was about to tuck him beneath the covers, when the door burst open.

"What's wrong?" Stan demanded, strain carving his features. "Is he all right?" He fastened the belt around his robe, but the material sagged across his chest, revealing the scatter of gold curls.

"Shh." Stella placed a forefinger on her lips and tried to ignore her pulse bruising her ribs.

He shook his hair off his brow, his drowsy gaze catching and holding her own. She held his greatest treasure in her arms. Swallowing, she bit her lip and tried to analyze her reaction to him. She couldn't. At that moment, the child stirred in her arms and put a stop to her troubling thoughts.

"What's up, sport?" Stan asked.

The boy snuggled closer to Stella.

"I see you're okay." He stepped nearer to help put him to bed, and his foot caught on the frayed mat. Toppling off balance, he grabbed for the bedside table, the lamp crashed to the floor and he followed.

Jarred awake, the child gaped at Stella, then at his father sprawled on the carpet. "Let go, witch." He pummeled her chest with his fists. "Witch!"

Stella let him go. He scrambled from the bed and knelt beside his father, crying.

"I'm all right, Troy." Stan shuffled to a sitting position and hugged him close. "Poppa's okay."

The scene tugged at her heart, and feeling like an intruder, Stella walked for the door.

"Hold it, Ms. Ryan," Stan said.

Stella paused, every nerve in her body tensing.

"Time you met my son, Troy." He pushed himself to his feet and whispered to the boy.

"Ho-ow do you do, Ms. Ryan." Troy drew closer to his father and clutched onto his pyjamas. Slowly, he stretched out his thin hand.

Stella reached out and the moment her fingertips brushed his, he snatched his hand back, hiding it behind his back.

"What's cracklin', Troy?" Stella smiled, and squatted to match the child's height. "Your room's cool, dude."

Intrigued, Troy stared at her but remained glued to his father's side.

Stella patted her hands on her thighs and stood. Her gaze skittered from the son to the father, and settled on him for a heartbeat.

An erratic beat.

A troubled beat.

She glanced down at her bare feet, then wished she hadn't. A blush warmed her cheeks. That, and the flimsy nightgown she wore made her feel vulnerable.

A distinct disadvantage.

Abruptly, she turned and walked away, the carpet cushioning her footsteps.

"We'll see you at breakfast, Ms. Ryan," Stan called after her as she slipped out the door.

An hour later, Stella bounced down the stairs to the dining room. She had to go without makeup, even lipgloss. She'd swept her hair up and fastened it in a ponytail with an elastic she found on the dresser. Unable to bring herself to wear her sweat-stained jogging suit again, she succumbed and slipped on the Karate gui she found on the bed that first day; the whisper of silk, a seductive caress over her body. The scarlet shade complimented her fair complexion. She tied the sash around her waist and chuckled. It'd be flashy in a tournament, but so inappropriate for working out. She preferred her well-worn guis and her hard-earned black belt strapped around her waist.

The instant she entered the room, Stella felt like a specimen under a magnifying glass. Both father and son gaped at her. She wiggled her shoulders and stood her ground.

"Perfect timing, Ms. Ryan." Stan rose from his chair, his gaze strobing over her silk-clad curves. "The uniform fits."

"Gui," she corrected, plunking down in the nearest chair.

"Independent to the hilt—" He resumed his seat, his muttered words for her ears alone.

"Have to be," she fired back, smiling to take the sting

from her words with the child still staring at her. "Especially these days" –she paused— "and in these circumstances."

He didn't miss her meaning, and she didn't miss the imperceptible narrowing of his eyes.

A warning?

Dismissing the thought, she turned to the boy dressed in corduroy pants and a sweater, sitting so proper in the huge chair, his slippered feet dangling over the edge. "You're looking pretty nifty in that outfit, Troy."

A timid smile flittered across his mouth. "My ... my poppa says" –he glanced at his father, then back at her— "you're here to teach me Ka-arate."

Stella shot a veiled glance at Stan. He shrugged, but his jaw tightened, his mouth set.

"I'd love to," she said, softly. "But I have to go back to work."

Troy's lashes fell over his eyes and he withdrew into his shell.

She could've clobbered Stan for maneuvering her into this. Perhaps one day she would, and how.

"Sensei Ryan has to return to teach her other students." Stan buttered a piece of toast and took a bite. "She doesn't have time for a lesson today."

He might as well have taken a chunk out of her instead of the slice of bread. The boy's crestfallen face jabbed at her heart. Guilt stabbed ... but she had nothing to feel guilty about.

"Your father can bring you to the studio." Stella twisted the napkin in her lap, imagining it to be said father's neck. "I'll show you some fast moves."

Stan cocked a brow.

Stella ignored him.

Troy nodded, but his lip trembled and his eyes shimmered with tears.

"That's very good of Ms. Ryan, son," Stan said. "I'm sure she'd like to know you root for her in tournaments to floor her opponent." Just try it, his eyes said.

Wicked man.

Wicked.

But his words brought a hint of a smile to Troy's mouth. The ogre had a saving grace after all. That irritated her more, because she couldn't use that excuse to dislike him outright.

"And how you gobble up *Sports Unlimited.*" He raised his cup and took a sip of coffee.

Troy's shy smile broadened, dimpling his cheek.

Top that, he seemed to challenge.

She did.

"I'd be honored to teach such a fan." Stella gripped the glass of orange juice between her palms. "You'd make a fine karateka."

A spark lit Troy's eyes, then quickly diminished together with his smile. He poked the scrambled eggs on his plate with his fork.

"You could show her your scrapbook." Stan set the coffee cup on its saucer with a definite clatter. "I'm sure Ms. Ryan would want to see it."

Stella bit her lip, not missing the subtle sarcasm underlying his words. Stan Rogers was playing an unfriendly game and she was determined not to fall prey to it.

"I'd be delighted to see it, Troy," she said, voice gentle. "I hope you'll bring it with you when you visit my dojo."

Stan leaned back in his chair and folded his arms across his chest, his eyes drilling into her.

Moments pulsed with tension, building to breaking point. An invisible cord seemed to wind itself around her heart, imprisoning her to him ... and a warning sounded in her head.

"Could I ... uh ... show you my picture book before you go, Ms. Ryan?" Troy asked, glancing at her from beneath his sooty lashes.

"I don't think Ms. Ryan has time for that, Troy," Stan said. "Even her weekends are booked. If she could, she'd spend this weekend with you."

Except it wouldn't be just with the boy. *It'd be with you too, you big bad wolf.*

Bad, bad wolf.

"Go ask Minni what time they're leaving." He pushed back his chair and stood, his glacial glare making her shiver. "Ms. Ryan's ready to go."

The child shuffled off the chair and trudged to the door, his head downbent.

Stella set the glass down and jumped up, almost knocking over her chair.

"How dare you," she murmured, her words tumbling from her mouth. "You had no right to disregard my wishes in that imperious way."

"Is that what you think?"

"That and a whole lot besides," she said, her ire reflected in her stance. The man was aggravating. The child adorable, currently rubbing his eyes with the cuff of his sleeve. Her heart jerked. As much as she tried to dismiss it, compassion for the boy overrode her fury with the father.

"Just a minute, Troy." She walked up to the child and placed an arm across his shoulders. He stiffened. Gently, she turned him round to face her and he relaxed a fraction. "I'd like to spend some time with you today." She dared a covert glance at Stan who stood with his arms akimbo and a mocking line slashed across his mouth. "I'll leave tomorrow evening instead and be back in time for my Monday classes. How's that?"

Troy's face lit up and he ran to his father, tugging at his trouser leg. "Can she stay, Poppa, can she?"

"Of course." Stan ruffled his son's dark curls with his hand, his eyes sparring with hers. "That was the idea

... to score.'"

Troy dashed from the room calling for Minni.

"I don't like being blackmailed, Rogers." Stella marched fast forward and halted, keeping the wide girth of table between them. So, he'd scored a hit at her expense. This tug-of-war between them was by no means over.

"Blackmailed?" He slapped his hands on the surface and leaned closer. "I don't blackmail anyone, Ms. Ryan. You chose to stay."

Stella gripped the edge so hard the weave of lace imprinted itself on her fingertips. "You staged that very well." Indignant, she met his gaze head on. "I'd call that emotional blackmail."

In a swift movement, he lurched around the table and pulled her hard against him. "Call it what you will."

"A spade's a spade, Rogers."

An amused line feathered his lips. "So it is."

Stella spread her hands across his chest to push him away.

Major blunder.

His sexual heat zapped into her fingers ... her bloodstream ... her heart. A gasp caught in her throat, and she let him go, staying frozen to the spot.

"Thanks for what you did for my son just now." He traced her lips with his thumb. "I like closing the deal my way."

56

Stella found her voice. "Two can play that game." She took a step back.

Breathing room.

"But there's only one winner."

"Depends on what game you play."

"And how." He considered her a moment, his mouth twitching at the corners. "A frontrunner—"

"You think it's you?"

A broad grin broke across his lips.

"Early leads set themselves up for a takeover."

A glint of surprise, then he squinted at her. "Time will tell."

"In the event of a tie?"

"Sudden death, of course." He wiggled his brows and his grin turned into a wolfish smile. "You should know that, Ryan."

"Rules?"

"Mine."

She laughed, the sound crackling with cynicism. "You controlling bast —"

"I wouldn't, Ryan," he advised. "There's a child in the house."

She would floor him one day.

She would.

But for now, she bridged the gap and risked shoving him back again.

He didn't budge. "If it wasn't for him, I ..."

"I know." He stalked past her and out of the room, slamming the door behind him.

Chapter 5

A couple of hours later, Stella stood watching Minni and the guys board the Hummer, her resentment directed at Stan who was giving them last minute instructions. She should've been on it. A heavy sigh escaped her, and she glanced over her shoulder. Troy had his face pressed against the living room window, his breath fogging the pane. She'd given her word to the child. She couldn't go back on it now, but within twenty-four hours she'd be out of here, conscience free.

When the Hummer began bumping along the track on its way to Vancouver, she glanced up at the sky. There were more blue patches than clouds. At least the weather was in her favor.

"Praying for a way out, already?" Stan walked towards her, the gravel crunching beneath his sturdy boots.

"Glad to see the Indian summer's holding," she said. "No snow for another month or so."

"Seems that way. However," he added with a wicked

grin, "looks can be deceptive."

"Well, they can remain that way until I get home."

He laughed and the sound ricocheted through the wooded glen.

"I'm sure I can find more pleasant company inside." She stomped through the entrance and shut the door to muffle the sound. It didn't work. His deep laughter sailed through, grazing her skin and settling somewhere in the vicinity of her heart. She groaned, and sought out Troy, thinking he'd distract her from his father's provocative presence.

Troy knelt on the couch and drew squiggles on the misty pane with his finger. She wondered what it was about this child that beckoned to her motherly instincts. Perhaps it was his lost, forlorn look. Perhaps it was her. Had she made the right decision focusing on her career over marriage? Of course, she had. All she had to do was look at the divorce rate.

Up until now, Stella hadn't met anyone who'd touched her soul, who'd made her heart race, who'd ... then she skidded, shocked, her hand flying to her mouth. She shook her head. Her world revolved around her business; his around his son. Not in a million years. She chuckled, dispelling the dangerous notion...

"Hey there, Troy." She forced a smile on her mouth. "Ready to show me your books?"

The boy slipped off the sofa and beckoned her to

follow him upstairs.

If spending a day with the boy helped pacify the father, then good. Should Stan nix her qualifying for affordable mortgage refinance rates, she could lose her business. She raised her chin a fraction and stiffened her back with resolution. The battle lines had been drawn and subtle as they were, there was no mistaking them. She had no intention of being ambushed again, verbally or otherwise.

"We'll see who wins, Mr. Arrogant Ogre," she muttered beneath her breath and trudged after Troy.

Twenty minutes later, Stella still sat on the floor of Troy's room while he flipped through his scrapbooks. When he pointed to a picture of her, they burst into a fit of giggles, and she had to wonder why he'd called her 'witch' in that disturbing way. However, before she could figure it out, she felt the now familiar sensation of fine down on the back of her neck standing on end ... and her head snapped up.

"Having fun, you two?" Stan asked, pausing in the doorway on his way to his office downstairs.

Stella swallowed her laughter and remained silent, a sliver of awareness spearing her. The man attracted her like a magnet and that made him a triple threat. To her heart, her mind ... her.

"Here's a funny picture of Sensei Ryan." Troy held up the scrapbook and giggled anew.

"No." Stella made a playful grab for it, but Troy waved it at his father anyway.

A jab of pain flared inside Stan. It was the first time his son had laughed in that carefree way, and it was because of the woman next to him. A ripple of unease shot through him. What would happen when she left? Unless, he—another whack to his conscience. Ruthlessly, he crushed the thought into oblivion. Troy should be laughing and playing everyday. Children supposedly laughed one hundred and fifty times a day, and adults one tenth of that. Maybe he needed to take the hint.

Stan smiled. "Nice tumble."

"What're you doing here?" she asked, wariness in her voice. "I thought you were working in your study."

"I came to get an account file from my room." He indicated the folder in his hand. "Your laughter gave me pause."

Stan allowed his gaze to travel over her and settled on the modest V opening of her gui top. The thin material outlined her breasts, her nipples straining against the soft silk. She'd fit perfectly in his hands, her skin velvet soft. He clamped down on his erotic thoughts and scrubbed a hand across his bearded jaw. Definitely, he'd take a ride into town as soon as Minni and the men returned. Time he viewed what the city had to offer. He'd shut himself up here far too long. That explained this foolishness regarding the woman under his roof.

"We're not laughing now," Stella said, the veiled sharpness of her words ripping into him.

"I see." He was no fool. Clearly, she was letting him know that although she'd agreed to spend the day with his son, she didn't welcome his company. A muscle pummeled his jaw. "Stella, come to my office at three. I want to discuss a few things with you." About to say something to his son, he changed his mind and stalked down the hall.

"Right, Stan." Stella jumped up and peered at him from around the doorjamb. "There are one or two things I'd like to discuss with you, too."

He paused in stride, his back rigid. "I'll look forward to it," he tossed over his shoulder, a sardonic twist to his mouth. "Don't wait for me with lunch. Minni left sandwiches and fruit in the fridge." He took a step down the stairs and brushed the bridge of his nose with his thumb. What could the woman want now, apart from the obvious? To get away from him.

"Oh, wait."

He turned and hiked a brow.

"I'd like to work out before lunch," she said. "I'm used to running in the morning and I missed it today. Is there some place I can jog?"

"Of course." He nodded. "There's the gym or the trails behind the house." For a long moment, he searched her features, trying to read her. "Don't get lost in the forest."

"Don't worry," she replied, tone dry. "I'm quite self-sufficient."

"In what areas?"

"All."

"I wonder." He scoped the length of her body, a flicker of a pause at her cleavage, and raised his eyes higher, connecting with her wary gaze. Instinctively, her hand flew to the modest neckline of her gui and she blushed. The movement, however, served only to further accentuate the fullness of her breasts.

Stan shuttered his gaze. "See you at three."

"You are the most infuriating man—"

"Feeling is mutual, ma'am." He inclined his head and sauntered off, chuckling. Sure, he'd scored another point on this nebulous duel between them. Yet, there was no joy in him for all that.

"Oh!" Stella slapped her hand over her mouth, smothering the sound, before she screamed in frustration. She was not a shrieking, emotional woman, but this man had her temperature rising with his verbal sparring, his midnight-blue eyes, his ... She was controlled, she was cool, calm and collected ... except when it came to him.

A snicker sounded behind her. She glanced over her shoulder at Troy grinning from ear to ear.

"What're you smiling at, kid?"

"I'm glad you and my dad like each other," he said

with youthful wisdom.

"You think so, do you?" She leaped for him and he shrieked in delight, dashing around the room away from her. "Come on, let's see the rest of this artwork of yours."

An hour later, Stella left the boy busy working on his martial arts project and strolled outside in search of a track. Air chilled her skin and she rubbed her hands over her arms. She would've liked a pullover sweater to retain body heat but since she was sparse in the clothing department, decided to grin and bear it.

She hopped from one foot to the other warming up and gazed up at the tall pines. Since this morning, the clouds had infused the sky with various shades of gray. She breathed deeply a few times and fresh, cool air filled her lungs. She started to run.

Stan stood by the window of his study and watched her take off. A free spirit. For the hundredth time, he wondered if he was doing the right thing by her. He rubbed a hand across his forehead. Of course, he wasn't. But he had the boy to think about. In the end, she'd be okay. Then, another thought stole through ... would he? Could he forgive himself? He heaved a sigh and trudged back to his desk, slumping in his swivel chair. He punched a key and booted up the computer.

Tension knotted his muscles, and he rolled his shoulders to ease the tightness. He drummed the desktop with his thumb and stared at the hardcopy file topping the stack. Finally, he picked it up and brushed his hand over the nametag. Stella Ryan.

*   *   *

Stella wove her way around the trails, icy air nipping at her nose and making her cheeks tingle. Working out was a lonesome event, but today an odd squirrel scurried by and kept her company. After about forty minutes, she slowed to a brisk walk to cool down and exhilaration surged through her. Humming a tune, she blotted perspiration off her brow with her sleeve and skipped up the front steps to the lodge.

Thirsty, she ambled to the kitchen, filled a glass with water and leaned against the counter, taking several sips. Next, a shower and change of clothes ... she wrinkled her brow. She had no clothes to change into.

"Finished already?" Stan pushed through the swinging doors and made her jump.

The water went down the wrong way and she sputtered.

Instantly, he lurched forward and patted her back. "Easy, Stella." He smiled, and her stomach took a dive. "You enjoyed your jog, I take it?"

"Ye-es, I did." She brushed a curl off her moist temple and took another sip of water. Cautiously, she swallowed, then coughed.

"You all right?" He reached out to pound her back but she pushed his arm away.

"Fi-i-ine," she wheezed, eyes watering.

He thought a minute, then grabbed a sandwich and an apple from the refrigerator and sauntered past her.

"Umm, where's the laundry?" she blurted. "I need to wash."

"Leave it for Minni," he tossed back through the wooden panel. "She won't mind doing it for you."

"I mind," she said, her voice rising. "I-I've got to wash. I don't have anything to wear."

He swerved back around the door. "I'll send Joe for your things."

"That won't be necessary for one extra day," she insisted. "I just want to wash my jogging suit, have something clean to wear the rest of the day."

"Of course, one extra day." He shrugged and pointed to the laundry facilities. "Please yourself." Throwing the apple in the air, he caught it and sidestepping the door, bit into a sandwich.

"Please yourself," she mimicked, pouring a few drops of water from the glass into her hand and rubbing her nape. Her rising temperature had nothing to do with the two miles she'd jogged. He made her blood boil, her heart race, her nerves bop. She sucked in a mouthful of air and it slipped out of her in a near whimper.

Not long afterward, she showered and dressed in her freshly laundered suit, her moist hair brushing her shoulders. She checked on Troy who was napping, and tiptoed back downstairs to the kitchen. She took a sandwich from the refrigerator and plopped down on a chair at the table, replaying the last couple of days in her mind. The moment the clock struck three, she put the last piece of cheese in her mouth and reluctantly pushed back her chair. Stalling for time, she washed the plate, placed it on the draining board and dried her hands on the towel hooked to the wall. She smoothed her damp hair over her temples and marched out to meet the lion in his den.

After a deep breath, she knocked on his office door.

"It's open," Stan called, his gruff voice filtering through the portal.

She turned the knob, stepped inside and paused, scoping the room. He was so absorbed in the open files on his desk that he hadn't even glanced up. His hair was ruffled, his shirt cuffs rolled to his elbows. Daylight filtering from the window behind him, made evident the deep grooves on his cheeks and snowy threads at his temples. Tenderness nabbed at her heart but she gritted her teeth, dismissing the invasive feeling. She reminded herself he was a ruthless businessman who held her future in the palm of his hand. If he decided to close his fist and squeeze, she'd be hard pressed to stay alive financially.

"Sit down, Stella," he invited, rubbing his neck with a strong hand.

"Relax, I'm not going to bite." Finally, he raised his head and the corner of his mouth tilted in a grin. "This time."

"Is there another?" she shot back.

He chuckled. "Might be."

"Not if I can help it," she muttered to herself, plonking down on the chair facing him. Ignoring her tripping pulse, she folded her hands in her lap and tapped her foot on the plush, chocolate-colored carpet.

Stan caught the wariness in her eyes and the angle of her chin, and his chuckle softened to a smile. Straight, damp curls framed her face devoid of makeup and gave her a little girl look. A direct contrast to the tough, street-wise image she tried so hard to portray. She really was charming, he thought. However, that could be deceptive in the female species as he'd found to his detriment. He'd not fall for it again.

"I see you found the laundry," he said, indicating her jogging suit.

"Yes."

"Would you like some coffee?"

"No."

"Sounds like this is going to be a one-sided conversation." He pushed his chair back, stepped across to the counter by the window and poured himself a cup of steaming brew from the percolator.

"Not at all," Stella replied, all business. "I prefer to delete any nonsense and get down to brass tacks."

"Right you are, Stella." He placed the mug on a coaster on the desk, reclined in the chair and toyed with a pen between his fingers. "Thanks again for staying to spend the day with my son."

It was not what she expected to hear but if he was willing to withhold tossing down the gauntlet, then so would she, with caution. She'd not be lulled into a false sense of security by his words of gratitude.

"The weekend doesn't interfere too much with my job." She paused for effect. "And you have ... er ... persuasive ways."

"But not convincing enough for you to take the job."

"Out of the question."

"Salary would double what you make at the studio in three months."

"How would you know?"

He raised an eyebrow.

"Of course, how foolish of me."

"I'm your lender. It's my business to review income and—"

"I won't forget again."

"I'm sure you won't."

"What is it you want, Rogers?" she asked, her words

cool. "I'm not interested in playing this 'gotcha' game with you."

"Nor I with you."

His eyes collided with hers. A quiver ripped through her. Unbidden, her hand moved to her stomach, but the action inside her was at full speed. Fight or flight was the decision she needed to make. Although tempted to leap up and get out, she steeled her nerves and stood her ground. But at the back of her mind another thought challenged. Was this more a personal than professional risk confronting her?

"What's your plan for Troy?" he asked, his tone a muted growl.

She refused to be baited and following his lead, played the soft touch.

"I'd like to take him through some preliminary lessons."

"The gymnasium's for your use." He nodded, acknowledging her silent nod to a temporary truce between them. "Karate will keep him busy, help him forget—"

"What?"

"Generate pleasant memories for him," he murmured, dodging her question.

"He's very keen." She pushed frustration aside, realizing that for the time being, her questions would go unanswered.

"Sure is." He scribbled on a pad, tore the check out

and handed it to her. "This should do for one day's work."

"Not necessary," she said. "This is my gift to Troy."

"Take it." He slid it across the desktop to her.

"I don't want it." She attempted to stare him down but he didn't even blink. "I'll accept payment for lessons at the studio, but not this one."

He hauled himself from the chair and skirting the desk, placed the check in her hands. "My gift to you."

"Hardly." She crumpled the check in her hand and hurled it at him. "Don't insult me." She leaped up and turned away.

A heated moment, he grabbed her by the shoulders, spinning her around to face him. "I wasn't insulting you. I wanted to express my gratitude for what you're doing for my son."

"I don't want your gratitude," she said, her words distinct. "I'm doing this for Troy, not you."

"Maybe you want me to show my thanks another way." He pulled her hard against his chest, his gaze blue flame and swooped down, taking her lips in a fierce kiss.

Just as quickly, he let her go, surprised, as she was shocked.

An explosive heartbeat, and he covered her mouth again, plundering with his tongue, his hands weaving through her hair. Stella met his passion, sliding her tongue over his, touching, tasting ... a waltz of the senses.

He groaned deep in his throat and kissed his way from her tremulous mouth along her cheek to her earlobe. He nipped, he breathed and fueled her nerves with sensation. Moving his lips a notch lower, he feasted on the pulse point at her throat. Then, he raised his head and ignited her lips once again with the erotic fervor of his own. Stella purred deep in her throat and curled closer to him, her fingers sliding through his hair in a frenzied tempo.

Gliding his hands around her midriff, he brushed her buttocks, and scooped her up in his arms; his breathing heavy. He stepped to the sofa and nestling her amidst the cushions, stretched out beside her. Cupping her breast in the palm of his hand, he flicked her nipple with his thumb. His mouth pressed to the curve of her cheek, her chin, her throat, and with each kiss, he inched the zipper of her sweatshirt lower. Finally, he lifted the abrasive material off her shoulder and lay claim to the spot with his lips, licking, nipping with his teeth.

She sucked in a breath, her body thrumming with acute sensation.

Kissing his way down, Stan paused at her cleavage and breathed in her sweet scent ... woman and fresh air. He explored and conquered. He licked her nipple, she writhed against him, and he took it full into his mouth, suckling. Dear God! Sweet torture. He swirled his tongue around the dusky tip, grazed the bud with his teeth and stroked it with his tongue. Heat fueled his blood. His heart pummeled his chest. His sex hard. His groan mingled with her moan of pleasure. She pressed her fingers into his shoulders, holding him to the spot ... passion binding him to her.

His hand replaced his mouth on her breast, and Stella squirmed, then sighed when he nipped her other nipple with his teeth, laving with his tongue. Heat spiraled inside her, melting her limbs, sensation coiled at the apex of her thighs.

"Stan," she gasped.

"Shh," he murmured, his breath heating her skin. "I-I-I want—"

Fever surged, and he pressed closer, his chest melding with her breasts. He raised his head, framed hers between his hands and ravaged her mouth with his.

"Dad!" The echo shot down the stairs and jolted them back to reality.

Stan heaved a breath, his lips still pressed to hers; Stella wriggled beneath him. He broke the kiss and traced her swollen lips with his thumb. Air buzzed with erotic energy, heat pulsed ... he held her gaze for another heartbeat, then let her go.

"Coming, Troy," he called, swiping hair off his brow. "Stella ..." He reached for her but she shook her head, avoiding his eyes.

Sexual awareness sizzled.

He muttered an oath and strode from the room.

A whimper filled her ears. It came from her. Trembling, she shuffled off the sofa, zipped up her sweatshirt and patted her hair in place. She touched her lips with her fingertips. A flush flamed her face. Whatever had possessed her to behave in that way? She didn't even like the man, did she?

After a pause, she plodded up the stairs and gripped the banister, lest her legs give out on her. When she drew close to Troy's door, her step faltered. She took a deep breath and her training kicked in. A best defense was an offense. She licked her lips, his taste still upon her mouth ... she moaned. Swallowing the emotion away, she stepped into the room.

Stan sat on the edge of the bed, watching Troy playing with toy cars, but the moment she walked in, he pinned her with his searching gaze.

Silence thickened, vibrating with unspoken innuendo.

Stella almost turned and ran. Almost. She'd never run from a challenge, and she'd not do it now. Even if this was different ... treading unchartered waters ... more dangerous. Fear and joy pulsed through her. Even if this challenge involved her heart.

"Come on, Troy," she said, plundering the silence, yet not looking at Stan. "Time for your first lesson."

While Troy dumped his toys in the box, Stan hauled himself up and stepped closer, sexual energy crackling between them. "You did very well for your first lesson, spitfire." He hooked a stray curl behind her ear.

His provocative words became the gauntlet he laid down, yet his tender touch confused her. Until she got clearance of what he was about, she could do only one thing. She picked up the gauntlet.

Chapter 6

Stella spent the next hour and a half with Troy in the gym behind the lodge. It included a sauna, a pool, a Jacuzzi and weight-training apparatus. Stan's regular work-outs explained how he kept in such good physical shape. As much as she resisted, her thoughts kept drifting back to the intimacies they shared in his office. His male scent seemed to have imbedded in her skin and his taste lingered upon her lips. The memory still had the power to make her go weak at the knees and catch her breath.

A nervous chuckle, and she shook her head at such utter foolishness.

"What's funny?" Troy sat cross-legged on the floor mat opposite her and wiggled his toes.

"Nothing, child." But was it? "Karate isn't to be used at random to spawn fights," she began, hoping to distance herself from her unsettling feelings. "But in defense of one's life and loved ones. Use it wisely and it will serve you well."

"Who started it?"

"The Chinese and Japanese people."

"Why?"

"Self-defense," she said. "But for a short time after World War II, some Martial Arts were outlawed in certain parts of Asia."

"Why?"

"Some leaders of the time feared they'd become militant—"

"I know what that means," he said. "Army stuff."

She grinned and nodded. "So, the masters, teachers—"

"Senseis," Troy said.

"That's right." Stella ruffled his hair. "Masters, skilled Martial Artists immigrated and brought Karate to North America and the world.

"What's Karate mean?" He tugged at his white T-shirt tucked into his navy shorts, his face enraptured with expectancy.

"Karate means empty hand." She pulled him to his feet and motioned for him to follow her lead. "It's defense without a weapon. Your body is your weapon."

"Oh, this is fun," he exclaimed. "I like it."

After a few combination moves ... punches, kicks, strikes and blocks, Stella led him through deep breathing exercises to calm and relax him. Soon after, she wrapped up the lesson. Troy stood and faced her, returning her brief bow; a sign of respect between teacher and student.

"Thank you, Ms. Ryan," he exclaimed, his hot face beaming.

"Sensei Ryan," she gently corrected.

"Sensei Ryan," he said and ran out, calling for his father.

Smiling at his eagerness, she strolled to the pool. The water beckoned, and impulsively, she threw off her clothes bar her bikini briefs and bra and waded in, the liquid cooling her body. After swimming several laps, she floated on her back, feeling relaxed and at peace. She squinted up at the skylight, blinked, and her tranquility shattered.

"Snow," she gasped, floundering. Quickly, she got her bearings and swam for the stairs to climb out.

"What's your hurry?" Stan leaned against one of the pillars that held up the roof, his legs crossed at the ankles.

Stella slid back into the water, an embarrassed flush fusing her body.

"How long have you been standing there?" She wiped chlorinated water from her eyelashes and trod water.

"Long enough." He allowed his eyes to roam over her, a grin playing on his mouth.

She sputtered and scooping up a handful of water, threw it at him.

Laughing, he wiped the droplets off his trimmed

beard. "You're in quite a predicament, my lady." He feigned a bow and bridging the gap, extended his hand.

"Get away." She threatened with a second handful of water. "How dare you spy on me."

"I wasn't spying." His hot gaze brushed her rounded curves and his grin broadened into a wide smile. "How was I to know I'd find a mermaid in my pool."

"What're you doing here?"

"Getting ready to go swimming with my son. Quite a lesson you gave him, Sensei." He winked. "Couldn't stop talking about it."

She treaded water like mad. "I want to get out."

"By all means." Stan waved his hand but made no move to leave, amusement twitching his lips.

"Are you going to stand there all day?"

"I find the view stimulating."

A hot flush invaded her body, seemingly impossible in the cool water ... she blinked at him. "Go away."

"Say, please turn around, Mr. Rogers."

She punched the water with her fist. "No."

Chuckling, he side-stepped the spray.

Oh, blast the man. Goosebumps lifted on her flesh and her teeth chattered. "All right." She sighed in exasperation. "Turn around ... please," she mimicked.

He arched a brow and stood his ground.

"You'll get yours one of these days, Rogers."

"Oh, I hope so." His eyes shadowed, and her heart

thrummed a dangerous tune.

Silence sizzled.

He leaned around the pillar, snatched a large white towel and held it open for her. "Come on out, princess, before you catch a cold."

"Turn your head."

He did.

Stella stepped out of the pool. "Tha-ank you."

Stan wrapped the towel around her body and held her in his arms a fraction longer than necessary. "Go get dressed," he said, voice gruff. He gave her a gentle nudge towards the changing room and followed her fluid movements with his shuttered gaze.

Her skin felt branded from his touch, and she quickly stepped under the shower in the hope of diminishing the effect. It didn't work, so she forced her mind to think about her return home. For sure, she'd throw out this smelly old jogging suit and buy herself a couple of new, jazzy outfits.

Home.

How sweet that sounded ... and safe. And at the moment, so far away. She wrapped the towel around her head turban style and hoped the snow would melt by tomorrow.

She stepped from the changing room and heard laughter echoing from the pool. She peeked. Troy was climbing over his father's broad back and he flipped him into the water. Spluttering, Troy surfaced and came at him. This time, Stan's strong arms held him at bay. Troy giggled and attempted to climb over them but slid off, splashing into the water.

An unbidden smile brushed her lips, then vanished. Danger.

The man she determined to keep at bay was all too human, and much too attractive. Her heart skittered. She dashed from the room and yanked the outside door open. Snow flurries smacked her in the face and she slammed the door shut. Tasting ice crystals on her lips, she marched back to the swimming pool, her ire flaring.

While Troy played in the shallow end, Stan swam to her and hauled himself from the water, his muscles contracting. He stood with legs apart and gazed down at her, droplets glistening upon his bronze skin, pale curls plastered to his chest.

Impulsively, Stella reached behind the pillar, grabbed a huge white towel and tossed it to him. "Cover yourself."

He laughed and the sound ricocheted off the walls. "It's snowing outside."

He blotted moisture off his face and slung the towel around his neck. "So it is."

"When're Minni and the guys coming back?"

"Not tonight."

"Why not?"

"Because it's snowing."

"I know it's snowing," Stella said, enunciating each word to hide the tremor in her voice.

"They telephoned about half an hour ago. Roads are a mess. Traffic jams all over the city."

"They are coming back?" she asked. "I want to go home."

"Couldn't say for sure. Depends on the length of the snowstorm and when the roads clear." He studied her. "Could be a few days or a few months."

"You know I wanted to leave."

"Yes."

"We're trapped here."

"Appears that way," he said but quickly reassured. "There's enough food and fuel to last us for awhile." He cupped her chin with his hand and gazed into her eyes. "What're you afraid of?"

"I'm not afraid of anything." She jerked her head away. "You planned all this."

"Whoa, there girl." He chuckled. "Could I help it if snow was in God's plan at this time." Thoughtfully, he scratched his fuzzy chin and glanced heavenward. "It fit my plans and I'm thankful."

"Ooo, you're the most infuriating man ..."

"You've said that before."

Stella took a step nearer and pushed him back toward the pool.

"No, you don't, kitten, you're coming in with me." Stan grabbed her arms and pulled her with him, crashing into the water.

Stella shrieked, thrashing out at him, and Troy's giggles blended in from behind.

"All's fair ..." Stan dunked her head in the water.

She spluttered up and splashed him in the face, "... in love and war," she finished his sentence to herself. But with them it seemed to be a continuous battle rather than anything else ... and she was glad as it acted as a buffer to what lay beneath their skirmishes. Something she resisted, and had to shut out.

Chuckling, Stan grabbed her, and she tried to swim away but her waterlogged suit weighed her down. She reached out and gripped the ledge to stop herself from going under.

"Sta-ay away from me," she gasped.

With a wicked glint in his eye and a crooked grin on his lips, he stalked her and pounced. She squealed and slapped the water, bombarding him with spray.

He ignored her onslaught and pushed through, lifting her into his arms. "You asked for it, champ."

For a moment, time stood still. He focused on her laughing mouth. A breath, a heartbeat, and he lowered his head taking her lips in a kiss that caused a tsunami inside her. He must have felt the jolt too, for he broke the kiss and abruptly set her on the cement floor.

Stella muttered a blue streak beneath her breath to cover the vulnerable moment. He dove into the pool, camouflaging his own reaction, and swam to his son playing with a toy boat at the opposite end.

Exasperated, Stella picked herself up and lifting her pant legs, trudged from the gym, puddles of water streaming behind her.

Upstairs in her room, she giggled at her reflection in the mirror. A drowned rat could look better. Then, she sobered. She was stuck in the middle of nowhere with a child and a man who was virtually a stranger. A man who rocked her world. A man who made her feel ... more.

Suddenly feeling drained, she collapsed on the edge of the bed. Stan stirred emotions in her that she didn't want to dwell upon. It was the way he looked at her, caressed her with his eyes in such an intimate way. When he'd held her in his arms during those brief moments in his study, it had been a revelation ... and now by the pool, a confirmation. This golden giant had touched her heart and she doubted she'd recover from this interlude even after she was off his mountain.

A damp spot began spreading on the bedspread. Sighing, she stood and peeled off her wet clothes. She froze. Something he'd said flitted through her mind, haunting. "*It fit in with my plans ...*" She racked her brains ... what else did he want with her? Shivers tore through her, and her teeth chattered. The sooner she left, putting this place and its occupants behind her, the better.

She picked up her clothes, stepped to the closet and stopped, a wry twist to her mouth. Except for the red gui she'd worn during her workout that morning and the soaked suit in her hands, she had nothing else to wear.

Deep in thought, she strolled to the bathroom, squeezed the excess water from her suit into the sink and hung it up to dry near the heat vent. An idea hit, and she hurried back to the bedroom. Pulling a sheet off the bed, she wrapped it around her body, sarong-style and secured it with a knot between her breasts. She felt vulnerable with her shoulders bare and her pink-tipped toes peeking beneath the folds, but she had no other alternative. Shrugging, she swept her hair high on top of her head and fastened it in a Grecian knot.

Hours dragged by. She couldn't stay hidden in her room, and by six o'clock, gnawing in her stomach had her shuffling downstairs to the kitchen. She lifted the hem of her mock-up gown and gingerly stepped through the swinging doors. Mouth-watering aromas assailed her, and she smiled at the domestic scene before her eyes.

"That's a neat costume, Ms ... I mean Sensei." Troy giggled. "Except, it's not Halloween."

"Costume nothin', kid. Necessary threads, these." She twirled around and modeled it. "But look who's talking." Minni's aprons hung loosely around their waists and on Troy, it reached to his ankles.

"Also of necessity, ma'am." Stan stepped to the stove and stirred a pot of soup. "Now, if you want to eat, grab a knife and start chopping."

"Smells good." She moved beside Troy and began dicing a celery stick.

"We too, are self-sufficient." With a glint in his eye, Stan paced back and positioned himself beside her, the cutting board between them. "Like the lady who won't let me forget how independent she is." He raised the knife and sliced a juicy tomato. "But is it always enough?"

Stella scooped a handful of celery pieces and dumped them in the wooden bowl. "For me, it is."

"We'll see," he whispered in her ear, slashing the knife through the French bread.

Stella tossed her head back and sidestepped him to the other side of Troy.

Stan chuckled. "By the way, if you want some clothes ..." He inclined his head to the bed sheet wrapped so intimately around her body, his gaze riveted on her shoulders. Smooth as satin. He could almost feel their silkiness beneath his fingertips, their taste ... He swallowed and averted his gaze only to stumble across her breasts straining against the material. Breath stalled in his throat, and he sucked more air into his lungs. In one swift movement, he could flick the sheet off her, scoop her up in his arms and bury his head in her bosom. Heat infused every muscle of his body—he was going hard. Abruptly, he slammed the knife on the table and turned to the refrigerator.

"We have enough carrots, Dad," Troy piped in, seeing the bunch in his father's hand.

"Oh, yeah."

Stella peeked at him from beneath her lashes. "You were saying," she prompted, "something about clothes."

Or the lack of ... his eyes locked with hers but he didn't voice the provocative innuendo. He tightened his jaw. He was not that far gone, no way. He'd have to get her off his mountain, pronto, before he did something he would later regret. Frigid air from the refrigerator slapped him in the face, and he came to. He shut the door and stepped back to the table.

"Check Minni's room. She won't mind if you borrow something." Almost indifferent now, he brushed his eyes over her slender figure. "The fit and style might be a problem, but you can improvise. You're a pro at that."

"Of nec—"

"I know."

She lifted the blade and brought it down on crisp

lettuce leaves.

"On the other hand, if Minni's clothes pose a problem" –he angled his head and raised an eyebrow— "you can wear one of my shirts and improvise with that."

Stella held the knife in mid-air, then lowered it, chopping all the faster. "That won't be necessary." Her skin burned beneath his intense gaze. The intimacy of wearing his shirts, enveloping her in his scent would send her ... no, absolutely, definitely not. What she needed to do was maintain her distance from him and keep a cool head. Yes, that would be wiser. She wanted to leave his fortress heart whole.

Huh! Fat chance. She paid the warning no heed.

"As you like," he said.

After Troy set the kitchen table, they sat down and savored hearty vegetable soup, chunks of buttered French bread, salad, cheese and fruit for dessert. It was a silent meal except for Troy's frequent outbursts regarding his lesson with Stella. He had them laughing and by the end of the last course, there was a cozy, party atmosphere, conversation flowing easily.

"Thank you, fellas." Stella cradled the mug of hot chocolate between her palms. "I can't believe I ate all that."

"A good appetite is a sign of good health." Stan reclined in his chair. "Apple?"

"No." She laughed. "Not another bite."

"Troy?" he asked, his eyes never leaving her face.

"Na-a-a." Troy pushed his chair back and jumped up. "Let's roast marshmallows, Dad."

Stella picked up her steaming mug, and accompanied Troy and his father to the library. A fire in the hearth blazed its welcome. She sat on the sofa, Stan hunkered down on the opposite corner from her and Troy stood drinking his cup of cocoa. Almost done, he gazed at them expectantly over the rim and burst out laughing. It was infectious and they joined in, the joyous sound enfolding them like a warm blanket.

"Where are the marshmallows?" Troy asked. "Come on, Dad, you know where Minni keeps her treats."

"She's changed hiding places on me." He smothered a chuckle, looking a little rueful. "Why don't you and Stella search the cupboards while I go out and get us three roasting sticks."

Stella slammed her cup on the coffee table, Troy and Stan picking up her cue, did the same.

"Last one's a roasted marshy." She scrambled up and hurried to the kitchen with Troy nipping at her heels.

"You're on," Stan called back.

Troy rummaged through the pantry and within minutes, emerged victorious, clutching a bag full of marshmallows in his hand. He dashed back to the library, Stella cheering him on, just as Stan strode in.

"We won! We won!" Troy exclaimed, stuffing a white

blob in his mouth.

Smiling at his son, Stan shook snowflakes off his hair and shoulders. "Brr ... sure is coming down out there." He placed three twigs on the table. "Winners get first choice."

After Troy grabbed a stick, Stan pierced a marshmallow with the second spear and held it out to her. "For you."

"Thank you," Stella whispered, a little flustered by his thoughtfulness.

"Mmm, yummy." Troy licked his sticky fingers and extending the stick over the flickering flames, singed four marshmallows. Unconcerned, he pulled them off two at a time and stuffed them in his mouth, smacking his lips. "That was good."

"It certainly was. Now it's time for bed, sport."

"Aww, Dad," Troy argued. "You and Stella haven't eaten your marshmallows yet. Besides, I'm not a baby. I'm eight years old."

"What a grand old age, m' boy." Stan ruffled his hair. "To bed."

Troy made motions of getting up while his father marched in front of him to the door. "Come on, son, I'll see you up."

"I'll clear the dishes," Stella murmured.

"No rush," Stan said. "I'll help you when I come back."

The last thing Stella wanted was to be alone with him. She worked quickly and just as she folded the tea towel and placed it on the kitchen rack, Stan walked in.

He glanced around the spotless kitchen. "You're a quick worker, Ryan."

She patted the towel in place and remained silent.

"About some things," he amended in a quiet voice.

Stella's head shot up and her eyes met his. Her heart pulsed off beat. His gaze darkened and he took a step nearer. Thick tension filled the room, seeming to draw her closer to him, imprisoning her.

Stella lowered her lashes and with unsteady fingers began removing her apron. "Look, Rogers—" Her fingers fumbled with the knot.

"I am."

"I'm in no mood to spar with you."

"Here, let me." He reached behind her back and covered her hands with his, putting an end to her inept attempts to untie the knot.

She smelled the subtle scent of his aftershave, fresh as outdoors. She felt his heat. She held her breath. Slowly, she raised her lashes and he slammed into her with the intensity of his gaze. She took a step backward, her pulse racing.

He moved a step closer.

She edged further back, bumping against the counter.

He advanced.

"No."

"Yes." He untied the ribbons and with one swift flick removed the apron and threw it behind him. Then, he encircled her waist with his arms and drew her closer.

Stella raised her hands to ward him off and her fingers splayed against his chest. Heat penetrated the material of his shirt and shot into her, throwing her emotions into a tizzy.

Stan lifted his hands to the nape of her neck and removed the pins from her hair. It tumbled down, a golden mass of curls trailing through his fingers. A breathless moment, and he cupped her face between his hands, gazing deep into her eyes, then a notch lower targeting her lips.

"You may not be in the mood for sparring," he whispered, "but you're in the mood for this." He bent his head and claimed her mouth.

On the brink of surrender, Stella found the will power to twist away, her knees almost buckling. "I didn't come here to entertain you, Rogers," she bit out, voice wrought with emotion, heart hammering against her ribs.

Stan drew in a sharp breath. "Your words tell one story, your body another." He skimmed his gaze over her, then turned away and strode from the kitchen.

Stella sagged against the counter, clutching the edge and sucking in mouthfuls of air. Her temples pounded, her mouth went dry and she licked her lips. Long moments later, she trudged up the stairs to her room and threw herself on the bed. Tears flowed down her face and soaked the pillow. She sniffed, wiped her eyes with the back of her hand and turned over, glaring at the ceiling. She didn't want to feel all tangled inside whenever he came near. She wanted her life on easy drive. Didn't want this man to overhaul her life's work, by one look, one touch ... one kiss.

At twenty-seven, Stella wondered if she'd made the right choices in life. She'd seen what marriage had done to her friends. The majority ended in divorce and most of the rest went from day to day, living an existence they didn't want, either from fear of being alone or feeling guilty because of the kids. Stella had no intention of falling into that trap. If and when she did marry, she wanted it to be with both eyes open, wanted to feel alive, truly alive with her man. A little voice prodded her mind. *Wasn't that how Stan made her feel, and wasn't that why she fought him so hard?*

She flicked a stray strand off her forehead, flipped onto her stomach and punched the pillow. She was wary of getting involved. Sure, she'd had boyfriends in the past; some had wanted to get serious, others had been out for a good time. She hadn't liked being pressured and constantly fighting to keep her virtue.

At present, she had no desire to complicate her life

with anyone, especially Stan Rogers. Her path had veered in a different direction than most and she used her energies to fuel her career, rather than to get her man. Perhaps one day the paths would cross. She didn't look forward to it, certain it would be explosive.

"Blast you, Rogers." She curled up, sniffed and pulled the bedspread over her quivering body. Shifting her head to a drier spot on the pillow, she closed her eyes and a lone tear slid down her cheek, then another.

Next morning, wind whistling through the trees awoke Stella. She dragged her eyes open and peeked at the window from beneath the covers. Snow blew against the misty pane. She smothered a yawn, pulled the bedspread under her chin and huddled in the warmth for a few more minutes.

A knock on the door startled her and she rubbed her eyes. "Who is it?" She patted her tangled hair in place and slid from the bed, clutching the sheet close to her bosom. She walked to the door, kicking the folds from her path.

"It's me, Ms. Ry ... uh ... Sensei," Troy said, his voice filtering through the wooden panel.

She opened the door a crack and peered at the boy's freshly washed face. Dressed in brown corduroy pants and a red pullover sweater, he stood in the hallway, gazing up at her. His small feet were wrapped in woolly slippers and she smiled, noticing how he rubbed one foot a little nervously on the floor.

"I've brought you a cup of coffee," he offered. "My dad thought you might like it."

"Thank you." She reached out and took the steaming mug from his outstretched hand. The man had a heart after all, maybe. She shook her head. The man had a heart of stone. Best she remember that and remain distant, aloof, detached. She'd stay out of his way and she'd survive this ordeal. Yes, she would, she must.

"My dad said to ask if you wanted me to show you Minni's room."

"Yes, that'd be nice." She sipped the coffee and leaned against the doorjamb for a moment. "Mmm, this tastes so-o good." She sighed and smiled. "I'll meet you in your room in about twenty minutes, okay?"

Eagerly, he nodded and dashed off.

Stella closed the door and stepped next to the heat vent on the floor. Warm air filtered through, toasting her toes. It took awhile for the room to warm up this early in the morning and she stayed there for a few minutes, savoring the bittersweet brew.

Finally, she set the mug on the dresser, tossed the sheet on the bed and shivering, walked to the bathroom. In no time at all, she'd showered and run a comb through her hair. Groaning at her puffy eyes reflected in the mirror above the sink, she splashed cold water over them and blotted them dry with a soft, pink towel.

Make-up would do the trick. She hoped Minni had a few creams and lotions she could borrow. Grimacing, she slipped into her old, still slightly damp jogging suit from her dunk in the pool. She took a moment to straighten the bed and then hurried out to meet Troy.

For most of the day Stella and Troy rummaged through Minni's closet. Troy giggled at her modeling antics and her wiggly toes. Finally, she found two dresses, and although large and much too short, she could hold them in place with a belt tied around her waist. Shoes proved more difficult, but if she didn't venture outside, she could get by with her battered running shoes, once they dried out.

She hadn't seen Stan at all, except once when he passed her in the hallway. He'd glanced at the bundle in her arms and with a curt nod, continued on his way. Which was just fine by her.

Early on Monday morning, before Stan and Troy were up, Stella ran her daily two miles in the gym, followed by an hour's workout. Afterward, she took a quick dip in the pool and ambled to the kitchen for breakfast.

Stan stood by the stove, flipping flapjacks in the air, while Troy very carefully poured orange juice in their glasses. It turned out to be a quiet meal, except for the satisfied sounds from Troy gobbling his pancakes.

"Slow down there, Troy, m'boy," Stan advised, an indulgent smile on his lips. He raised his cup, took a sip of coffee and leveled his sights on Stella. "I'm going to hike to the parking area near the road today. I'd like to see what condition the truck's in after the snowfall."

"Can I come too, Dad?" Troy piped up, syrup dribbling on his chin.

Stella hid a smile.

"No," Stan said in a firm tone. "It may be dangerous, and wipe that sticky stuff off your chin."

Stella shifted in her seat.

"Concerned for me?" he asked her.

"Don't take it personally." She lowered her lashes, camouflaging what her eyes might reveal. "I'd be concerned for anyone who traipsed out in that snow-covered and pot-holed trail." A pause to control her emotions, and she flashed him a cool gaze.

"I see." He studied her for a few seconds and pushed his chair back. "Keep an eye on Troy for me, will you?"

"Of course," she said, but he'd already stomped through the door. A tense breath staggered from her, and she contemplated the dark liquid in her cup.

Stella filled the morning hours by flipping through magazines with Troy in the library. About an hour before lunch, she gave him a lesson in the gym, and laughed when he, too, asked the familiar question.

"How long will it take to get my black belt?"

"It could take from two to five years, depending on how often you work out and how you view Karate," she said. "It's an art form."

"What happens after I get my black belt?" He flicked out a front kick, excitement shining in his eyes.

"Then, my young karateka," she said, "is when you really begin to learn and understand the wisdom behind Karate. It's the beginning of the long journey to Shehan."

"Master?"

"That's right." She threw a punch at him.

He stepped back and blocked it.

She smiled. He was catching on fast.

Later that afternoon, after Troy lay down for a nap, Stella hurried back to the library. She stopped in her tracks. A cell phone was on the alcove by the window. Stan must've forgotten it there, accidentally or on purpose? Didn't matter. She could make use of it ... call someone, but who ... one of her friends ... and tell them what ... that she'd been kidnapped ... that wasn't entirely true ... and she didn't feel in any real danger.

Except maybe to her heart.

Stella stepped closer, her hand hovering above the phone. A deep sigh, and she stroked the receiver, the metal cold and smooth beneath her fingertips. She was about to flip it open, when it jingled. Startled, she jumped back. It rang for several seconds, and finally she lifted it to her ear.

"He-ello."

"Hello, hello," an impatient voice spoke from the

other end of the line. "Give me, Stan Rogers."

"He's not available," Stella said, hair on her nape rising. "Is there a message?"

"No." A heavy moment, and then the woman's words crackled through the airwaves. "On second thought, yes. Tell him it's his adoring wife.

Chapter 7

"Wife?" Stella gripped the receiver, blinking rapidly to banish the blackness from her eyes, the emptiness from inside her.

"That's right," the woman repeated. "Tell him I want to see him. He'll know what I mean." She gave a husky laugh and hung up.

Static sounded in her ear, and slowly Stella flipped the cell off. Chills crawled up her spine, numbing her. Stan was married. Yet, he wore no ring, and his behavior hadn't been that of a married man. A sharp sound left her stiff lips ... more fool she. Nausea churned in her stomach.

She heard a muffled sob and turned, the flash of red darting out the door snapped her into action.

"Troy!" She jogged after him. "Troy, wait!" By the time she got to the hallway, he was gone. After a hasty search, she rushed back, re-checking all the rooms on the main floor. He was nowhere to be seen.

Stella sprinted to the gym. A sigh of relief burst from her lips at the sight of the clear surface of the pool. She trotted back to the house and uncertain of what to do, paced the hallway.

"Stan, where are you when I need you?" She ran a hand through her mussed hair and a moan fluttered from deep within her. As much as she denied it, this man had become an integral part of her life. But she had to nip it now. End it. But first she had to find his son.

Where was Troy? A thought flashed through her mind and a feeling of unease gnawed her insides. She grabbed Minni's coat from the wall hook, draped it over her shoulders and hurried outside.

"Troy!" She searched the garage, then the woods surrounding the lodge. Panic clawed her nerves. Could someone have taken him? Was he out there in the bush? Dusk was settling and it was getting colder by the minute. Although it had stopped snowing, the air was icy crisp, the snow deep. And what of the wild animals ... a little boy lost in a dark forest. A whimper squeezed from her mouth, and she wrapped her arms around herself, pulling the coat closer about her.

Soaked to the knee, she trudged back to the verandah and paused a moment to contemplate her next move. A sharp sound burst from her and she ran inside taking the steps two at a time. She rushed into his room and flung the closet door wide open. Relief washed over her. His coat and boots were still there. He couldn't have gone far.

A sinister image flashed in her mind. She pressed her fingers to her pounding temples. She hadn't seen any footprints in the snow. If the child was carried out, he'd leave no tracks in the snow. Any others could have been brushed away with a branch. Shivering, she paced the floor, her snow-soaked sneakers squelching. When she heard the front door click, she flew out and down the stairs.

"Troy, is that you?" She leaped off the last two steps and smacked into Stan stomping through the door.

"Steady there." He gripped her shoulders, checking her headlong rush and booted the door shut. Glimpsing the distraught look on her face, he steeled his hands on her flesh. "What's going on?"

"I-I-I don't know."

"What d'you mean?" His eyes turned blue granite. "Where's my son?"

Stella blinked at tears trembling on her lashes and began an incoherent explanation.

"All right, all right." Stan pulled her into his arms. "Start again, from the beginning. I want the whole story."

The warmth of his embrace penetrated the panic gripping her and words tumbled from her mouth.

"Troy couldn't have gone far." He released her, his mind seeming miles away, his jaw sharp. "He wouldn't. Knows better." He frowned. "You searched everywhere?"

"Yes. Upstairs, downstairs, outside, the gym, the pool ... all over."

"Troy has been drilled not to go near the water on his own and without a key he can't ..." His shoulders drooped as if a heavy weight had landed on him. "Still, we'll have another look." He seemed to look right through her. "Check upstairs once more, while I retrace your steps outside."

After inspecting the top floor, Stella peered behind the shower curtain in her bathroom and felt deflated. She retraced her steps, leaned out the window but Troy wasn't crouched on the roof as she'd imagined ... hoped. She scanned her bedroom. If she were a child, where would she hide?

A flutter of hope.

In two seconds flat, she crossed the floor, knelt down and peeked under the bed, squinting at shadows. She heard a whimper. He was curled up like an abandoned puppy in the far corner.

"Troy." She reached out, brushing his shoulder with her fingertips but he jerked away. "Hey there, young karateka," she said, in a gentle, firm voice. "Come out. Your father and I have been looking for you."

"Don't want to."

"Honey, come here." She lay flat on her stomach so he could see her. "You know I love you."

"No, you don't. That's wha-a-at she said and ... and ..." He hid his face in the crook of his arm. "You'll leave too."

"I will not leave you, Troy." She bit her lip in frustration. Now, why had she said that? "Come here, I have something for you."

He turned and gazed up at her with his big blue eyes. "Wha-at?"

Stella stretched and touched his hand. When he didn't pull away, she helped him crawl out and onto her lap. She wrapped her arms around him and he burrowed his tear-streaked face on her shoulder, his small arms encircling her neck, his body shaking.

"It's all right, Troy. No one will hurt you again."

"What we-ere you going to show me," he asked in a sleepy voice.

"This." She hugged him close. "I love you." The confession startled her, and her heart hitched, realizing she meant it.

"Love you, too," he mumbled and lowered his damp lashes.

Stella balanced him in her arms and was about to stand, when the sound of a footstep made her glance up. Her eyes locked with Stan's and a million unspoken messages passed between them. In two strides, he reached her, lifted his son from her arms and carried him out.

A sigh of relief slipped from her lips, and Stella pushed off the floor and followed him into the bedroom. She turned back the covers and Stan settled his son in bed, smoothing a dark curl off his brow. She arranged the blankets around the child and brushed her lips to his forehead.

An emotional moment pulsed, and Stan took her hand, leading her to the hallway. "I could use a cup of coffee."

"I'll put the kettle on." Stella slipped her hand from his grasp and hurried ahead, he a step behind her.

After Stan set mugs on the table, he straddled a chair and steepled his hands in front of him. When chicory aroma permeated the kitchen, Stella picked up the pot and filled the cups with steaming liquid. She placed the pot on its stand and sat on the chair opposite him, her insides squelching.

"What're you thinking?" he asked, his voice a ripple in the quiet.

"It's nothing."

"Unusual."

Not biting his verbal bait, she leapt up and reached for the pot. "Would you like another cup?" Absurd, she'd just given him a cup full. *What was the matter with her? The man sitting in front of her ... that's what was the matter.*

"This is fine." He lifted the cup to his lips, studied her over the rim and took a sip. Carefully, he set the cup back on the saucer. "Time you knew something about Troy's background since you'll be staying awhile."

"What're you saying?" Stella sat back down on the chair, gripped her coffee cup with both hands and cast him a wary glance.

"Until the snow ploughs work their way up here, the road is blocked." He took another gulp of the now lukewarm coffee and gauged her reaction. "Doesn't look like they're going to make it for some time."

"How long might that be?"

"Hard to say. They're swamped cleaning city streets and freeways."

"Oh, great going!" She jumped up and turned on him. "At the first sign of clear roads, I'm off this blasted mountain."

"Got it." Stan saluted her with his cup. "You made that quite clear from the moment you got here." He took a drink and set the cup down.

"That's right." She twisted away, then back again. "This wouldn't have happened if you'd behaved like other men and come to the studio, instead of ... instead of ..." she said, voice faltering.

"I'm not other men," he bit out, savageness in his words. Hauling himself off the chair, he snared her shoulders between his hands and slammed her hard against his chest. "I do things my way. You'd better understand that right now."

"You made that crystal clear." She pushed at him. "Four years ago."

He narrowed his eyes, but didn't budge.

"You threaten, manipulate, insult, blackmail, maneuver ..." Stella paused for breath, her chest fueling with pent-up emotion, her nipples grazing his chest.

Sexual combustion sizzled.

"Wrong." He let her go and pressed his hands behind him on the table. "You imagined the worst of me."

"Don't try to side step the issue," she snapped, breathing easier now that space separated them. "It wasn't my imagination working overtime when you mentioned my mortgage renewal terms."

"An empty threat." He shrugged. "It worked."

"You're one choice bast—"

"Tsk, Tsk," he cut her off. "Seems you coined me in those colorful terms several times over."

She swallowed her wrath but her tone told a different story. "Then, you couldn't have eclipsed my mortgage terms?"

"Not couldn't, wouldn't." He straightened and folded his arms across his chest. "When I found Troy virtually dropped on my doorstep, I sold the Los Angeles firm, liquidated those assets and relocated."

"Here." Stella waved her arm about. "The mountain top."

He inclined his head.

"Catch?"

He cocked an eyebrow. "I wanted a schedule that allowed me more time with my son, and a lifestyle that kept the media sharks off my tail."

"You're protecting him—"

"Of course."

"What else," she asked, her words more a statement than a question. Whether it was a concrete high-rise or a pine-studded mountain, he was still head honcho. And where did that leave her? Floundering, that's where.

He chuckled at her astuteness. "I retained control of the New York branch—"

"The pulse of the network," she blurted, filling in the blank.

"And ... er ... certain choice contracts."

"Mine."

"Plus a few others, and several overseas."

"That's premeditated, underhanded ..." She stopped at a loss of words.

He snaked an arm out and caught her shoulders, his eyes warring with hers. "Although influential I am, heartless, I'm not."

"I wouldn't bet on it," Stella muttered, twisting from his grasp.

He chuckled, but it didn't quite reach his eyes.

"I should have called your bluff."

"A more experienced businessperson would have."

"I'm fast gaining in that department," she stated flatly.

Stan tossed back his head and laughed all the harder.

"Tell me something, Rogers," Stella asked, curiosity getting the better of her. "If I hadn't stayed after meeting Troy and it hadn't snowed, what would you have done?"

"There're other ways to play a winning game." His tone smooth, cunning, his gaze assessing. "Especially with a woman."

"You ... you're—"

"You leave me no doubt as to your estimation of my character," he bit out, his words clipped. "However, it's inevitable we'll be spending some time together and therefore, civility's in order." He sat down and glanced at her mutinous face. "Now, how about another cup of coffee."

Get it yourself, you pompous a-- She compressed her lips, fracturing that thought. What she wanted was to clobber the man, not be nice to him.

However, it'd be pointless to continue arguing over something neither of them had any control of at this time.

"All right," she muttered, reaching for the coffeepot.

"About my son." He stretched his hand across the table and covered hers.

She gripped the pot's handle tighter, her fingers quivering beneath his, her heart tumbling in her chest. "I've wondered about his behavior, moods, especially today." She withdrew her fingers from beneath his and placed both hands in her lap, the heat of his touch pulsing into her.

"That was Troy's mother." A dark shadow stormed across his eyes.

"I know," she whispered. "He heard me on the phone."

Stan rubbed a hand over his eyes. "What you don't know is that she wants him back."

"Can she?"

"She can," he said with resignation. "If I don't agree to her demands, she'll contest."

Stella wrinkled her brow.

"And being the mother, gives her an advantage."

"Not always," Stella said. "Sometimes full guardianship is awarded to the father." Enough of her friends had gone through this circuit, giving her the freeze on marriage.

"Sometimes?" Stan queried, his words heavy with cynicism. "After the hell he's been through, I want a sure thing ... I want custody of my son."

"He's here now—"

"A temporary arrangement until the court hearing ... papers signed." Stan smashed his fist on the table and made her jump. "In the meantime, she's stacking the deck in her favor and playing me for all I'm worth." He pushed the chair behind him, every muscle in his body taut. "It's a case of a married mother against a single father."

"Married," Stella echoed, relief washing through her.

"Six months ago she hooked an attorney." A humorless sound slipped from his lips but didn't hide the vulnerability in his eyes. "She unloaded the child on me and now the honeymoon's over, she's back to unsettle him."

"You have good counsel?" Stella asked, but it was more a statement than a question, knowing that a man like him would be good and prepped.

"Top solicitor firm in the country." He shoved a hand through his hair. "However, being married can work for her. The court will favor her over a single father." A heavy pause. "The kicker is that she doesn't really want the child."

"Are you sure?" Stella asked, unable to believe how anyone could not want that beautiful boy.

"It'd cramp her style." A harsh sound rumbled from deep in his throat. "Since he's been here, she's made no effort to contact him." About to sit again, he changed his mind. "I will not have that woman do another number on him." He paced the kitchen like a caged lion.

Stella gulped, pitying the other woman.

"I gave her a hefty enough settlement, but she squandered it. Paris fashion, Monte Carlo gambling—" He broke off, pain slashing his features.

In between playing musical chairs with her gigolos, she had my son," he snarled. "My son tossed from babysitters to boarding school to strangers like nobody wanted him. She though, didn't miss a beat jetting the globe for a good time." A nerve jerked his cheek. "I could wring her scrawny neck."

Stella gaped at him, and he glared, reading her mind.

"He's mine. DNA." His mouth softened, then hardened. His son would have a father, he'd make sure of it. It'd be far removed from what he, Stan had endured in his own childhood. He'd turn the world upside down to prevent her from getting to Troy, even if he—

"Why didn't you fight for custody before?"

"Because I ..." In a helpless gesture, he dropped his arms by his sides and sagged in the chair. "A raincheck on that." He took a deep breath and exhaled a heavy puff of air. "But I'll take that other cup of coffee."

Stella nodded and refilled his cup with the hot brew.

"Thanks," he murmured, noting the slight quiver to her hand. Her scented warmth wafted to him, then got lost in the overpowering flavor of the steaming coffee.

Could he go through with it? Go through with what he'd planned for her? *Plotted.* A jolt shook him. *Guilt?* He zeroed in on her mouth. His gut clenched. Her lips parted slightly as she drank her coffee. He ached to cover them with his own, tasting her ... stroking her skin, running his fingers through her hair. A rumble rose inside him—it wasn't guilt, it was another emotion, one he had to snuff out.

He couldn't afford going soft on her. By the time this was over, no matter how he played it, she'd end up hating him.

She glanced up, her eyes clouded with concern ... for him? *You are one choice bast*— He savagely locked down that accusation.

His close scrutiny made her blush. The cup rattled on the saucer, and she stood, stepping to the sink.

"No, you don't." He leaped from his chair and checked her. "Look at me, Stella." Placing his hands on her shoulders, he turned her to face him. Stella lifted her lashes sure he could see right into her soul. "If you've quite finished," she murmured, breath pocketing in her throat.

"Not quite." He swooped down and caught her lips with his own.

Stella met his ardor, kissing him back full force. He deepened the kiss for a heartbeat. Abruptly he pulled away, brushing her tremulous mouth with his thumb, his eyes shadowed. Wobbly, she reached behind her and gripped the counter for support.

"Thanks for lending an ear, honey girl." He stroked

her cheek with his forefinger, paused like he was unde-cided about something, then turning, marched out.

Stella stood in the middle of the kitchen with an empty coffee cup in her hand and the bittersweet taste of him on her lips. It seemed every time she had a conversation with him, she was left hanging, her head whirling with questions.

Inhaling, she filled her lungs with oxygen. Good. She didn't feel so lightheaded. Setting the cup and saucer in the sink with a resounding clatter, she exhaled in force and stomped through the kitchen door. Sure she'd clash with the lion again before the night was over.

Chapter 8

Stella plodded up the stairs feeling like weights were strapped to her shoulders, but still managed to peek in on Troy snoozing.

"Poor kid," she murmured, tiptoeing away to her room. "He must be emotionally exhausted." Taking a cue from him, she crashed down on her bed, her body buzzing with tension, her mind fuzzy, her heart thumping.

Although she'd caught a glimmer of Stan's reasons behind his actions, a puzzle piece still dangled. She had to know where it fit ... how *she* fit into all this. Sure as heck, her being Sensei to his son wasn't the whole picture.

She shuffled from the bed, kicked off her damp sneakers and slogged to the bathroom. She ran a bath, minus the bubbles, pinned her hair up and tossed her clothes on the floor. Steam swirled about her, and she dipped her toe in the water. Ah, perfect. She sank into the water, the warmth soothing her chilled body and dissolving the lead from her shoulders. A sound, half agony, half bliss flitted from her lips. She closed her eyes.

Moments later, she got out of the tub and snatched a towel from the chrome bar. After drying herself, she dropped it on the heap of clothes on the floor. She'd wash them later.

Stella stretched, touching her toes and on the way up, glanced out the window. Snow blanketed the ground and icicles dripped from the snow-laden pine branches.

"Brr." She shook her shoulders and slipped on Minni's over-sized white blouse and a gaudy-colored skirt. A pair of old socks Troy had given her warmed her feet.

She twisted her arms behind her, trying to fasten the buttons of the blouse when a knock sounded. By the time she stepped to answer it, Stan had walked in.

"Do you usually barge into a person's bedroom?" Stella snapped.

He grinned. "I did knock."

"You could've waited until I answered."

"I could've." He stepped closer, took her shoulders and propelled her around. "Here let me."

"No." She turned away and stepped back, bumping against the window ledge.

"Yes." He bridged the gap in one stride, and began to button her blouse. His fingers brushed her skin, and heat spiraled inside her.

Her back went rigid. Her breath expanded in her chest.

At last he lifted his hands ... she exhaled ... he pressed his palms over her shoulders ... and she sucked in air.

"Relax," he breathed the word in her ear, tickling her nerve endings.

She pushed him away.

"All right." He raised his hands, skimming her head to toe with his eyes, amusement lurking in their depths. "Where did you get those socks?"

"Not funny," she told him, indignant. "I don't like looking frumpy."

"Charming." He chuckled. "You're wearing my old red socks."

Stella stomped to the bed, snatched a pillow, took aim and landed him a wallop on the side of the head. "Get out."

"Not yet, lady."

Stan tossed the pillow back and the impact knocked her off balance.

She tumbled on the bed. He followed. Arching backward, she grabbed the other pillow and hurled it at him. He caught it, threw it back and pounced. Stella giggled, rolled over to the other side and shuffled away from him.

"Sly and wily, too." Stan chuckled, but a pillow

whacked his face, muffling the sound.

He retaliated ... Stella warded off his attack ... he tackled her onto the bed. Trapped under him, she tried to wiggle from beneath him and froze. His eyes challenged ... her stomach flipped and she swallowed her laughter.

A magical mood vibrated between them. He lowered his mouth and took her parted lips in a kiss that shook her to her toes. He followed with mini kisses to her ear, nuzzling the tender spot, his hand stroking the nape of her neck. A brush of his fingers, and the blouse slipped off her shoulder, his heat charging into her. His mouth settled on the curve of her shoulder, then he nibbled his way to her breasts.

He flicked one nipple with his thumb, courted the other with his tongue, then took the dusky tip full into his mouth. A purr of pleasure sounded in Stella's throat. She slid her hands beneath his shirt, his muscles hot and hard beneath her fingertips.

A husky sound from him, and he retraced the path to her lips, pillaging with his tongue, his breath mingling with hers, her tongue frolicking with his. Heaven. The kiss lengthened ... deepened. She arched against him, giving him kiss for kiss, her fingers slicing through his hair. He devoured every sweet inch of her and pulled her closer, his arousal pressing the apex of her thighs. A sigh of pure bliss feathered from her lips onto his, and he cupped her buttocks slamming her against him.

A grunt of desire, and he pulled her down on top of him, his mouth fused with hers, his hands fondling her curves. He slid his hands to the waistband of her skirt; a flick of his fingers and the fabric shimmied down her hips, pooling at her ankles. She kicked it off, her slender legs a vision to his hungry gaze. His fingers fluttered on her thighs.

He touched, he stroked.

She squirmed, she sighed.

A breathless break between kisses, and his brooding eyes connected with hers, signaling his need for more. She dug her fingers into his shoulders, drawing him closer, accepting his invitation ... sweet sensation shooting through her.

Stan groaned his pleasure.

Stella moaned her delight.

"I want you," he murmured against her lips, his voice husky. "I've wanted you for so—"

"Yes." Stella fumbled with the buttons of his shirt and he placed his hands over hers, helping her. When her fingers stumbled to his belt, his hands glided beneath the strip of lace across her hips.

A moment of awe...

"You're beautiful," he murmured, a catch in his voice.

"You're big." She blinked at the hard strength between his legs, fascinated.

He smiled and settled her beneath him.

Hot. Breathless. Erotic.

He held her tight, rocking her against him.

"Mmm." Stella sighed, feeling like she was finally home.

"Yes," he grunted, holding her like a masterpiece entrusted to him.

Stella trailed her hands around his navel and upward, teasing golden fuzz on his chest.

"Ouch." Stan nipped the corner of her mouth with his teeth.

She smiled against his lips and shifted, kissing her way down his torso, her tongue flicking his hot skin.

He sucked in a breath, blew it out in a puff of pure sexual energy and slid his hands across her back lifting her back up to him. Velvet … silk … endless. His hands swerved around her midriff and up, fondling her breasts, his tongue licking each tip.

He drew each into his mouth, suckling. Sheer delight. A purr deep in her throat, and she pressed against his hardness.

A groan, and he burned kisses across her cleavage, along her neck to her mouth, brushing her parted lips with the tip of his tongue. He outlined her lips, teased, tasted and finally covered them with his own. His heart thundered in his chest, his breathing heavy. He explored with his hands, every curve, every crevice of her body

... his kisses longer, deeper.

"Stan," she gasped.

"I know, baby," he breathed, inching his way to the shadow between her thighs. His fingers stroked her ... she was slick and moist ... ready.

A suspended beat, and positioning himself above her, he slid his sex inside her warmth. Heaven. He filled her, she was tight ... he bumped into an infinitesimal barrier.

A split second pause.

Stella whimpered, holding him to her.

He thrust deep, and caught her cry with his mouth. She dug her fingers into his shoulders and called his name. He began moving inside her. Perspiration poured over him. He plunged deeper, higher, taking her with a passion foreign to him. His rhythmic thrusts lifted her to the pinnacle and him with her ... held there ... tension built ... coiled tight ... exploded. Wave upon wave of sensation ripped through Stella ... he felt his own body convulse with ecstasy ... he gripped her to him, not letting go.

Scents of love enveloped them to the deep melody of their breathing. He brushed a moist tendril off her brow. She stroked a damp curl at his temple.

"Why didn't you tell me you'd never—" He pressed a quick kiss on the tip of her nose ... her chin ... her mouth.

"Would it have made any difference?" She lowered

her lashes, shy.

Stan raised her chin, willing her to look into his eyes. "You've honored me with that special gift."

"Thank you for saying that."

"Did I hurt you?"

She shook her head, a smile dancing on her mouth. "You were amazing."

"You too," he murmured, voice gruff. He stole another kiss, came up for air and winked. "A natural."

She playfully slugged his shoulder with her fist.

"Only with the right man," he whispered. "Me." He covered her mouth in a kiss that had her nerves buzzing and her heart singing.

Finally, he lifted his head and growled in her ear, "I'd better get you dressed, Sensei."

"I-I can do it, thanks," she whispered, a hint of shyness in her voice.

"S' long as I get to do the undressing part." He grinned, and slipped into his own clothes.

She smiled and turned her back for him to button her blouse.

"You must find an easier blouse to fasten or unfasten," he growled in her ear.

"Oh, get out of here," she said, her words tempered with tenderness.

"That's what you told me about" –he glanced at the Swiss watch on his wrist— "an hour ago, although not in quite the same way." He grinned, wiggling his brows.

Stella picked up a hairbrush from the dresser, threatening to throw it at him.

"All right." He laughed and trotted for the door. "I'm going."

"Oh, wait," she called. "What did you want when you barged in here?"

Stan arched an eyebrow, his eyes twinkling with mischief.

A blush crept up her neck, warming her cheeks.

"I wanted your help," he said, tone serious. "I'll speak to you about it after dinner." He pressed his lips to the crown of her head and stepped out the door.

Stella slammed the brush back on the dresser. He'd done it again.

Breezed out and left her wondering. She caught her reflection in the mirror. She glowed. A smile curved her lips.

Two days ago the only thing that mattered to her was her business. But since this giant of a man exploded into her life like a thunderstorm, she knew her world would never be the same. She loved him. Dear God! How had it happened? Even the thought of him had her pulse skyrocketing. She was still the same independent, strong-willed woman, but loving him lifted her to a new dimension in her life. It was good. Very, very good.

With a spring in her step, Stella poked her head in Troy's room, but not seeing him there, she bopped down the stairs. She paused at the bottom to pat her hair in place and strolled to the library.

"Who's winning?" She fixed her eyes on the checkerboard, instead of the man.

"I am," Troy piped up, kneeling on the carpet and propping his elbows on the coffee table.

"Way to go, young karateka." She smiled. "Feeling better?"

"Yes, thank you, Sensei." His eyes lit up at the acknowledgment, 'karateka.'

"Gotcha! Crown my man." Stan chuckled, rubbing his hands.

"Oh, Dad. That's not fair. I wasn't looking."

"Teach you to keep your eye on the game and not on the pretty girl."

He ruffled his son's dark curls and winked at Stella. "Wanna game, pretty lady?"

"Maybe later. I thought I'd get something started for dinner."

"We got pizza in the oven." Troy giggled and captured two of his dad's men.

"In that case, I'll pace your game." She curled up on the sofa, her gaze straying to the man hunkered on the carpet. Firelight glinted on his hair, emphasizing the silver threads at his temples. Not an hour ago, she'd ran her fingers through the silky softness and ... even the memory gave her a rush. "I-I like to see what my competition's going to be."

"Is that so?" Stan joked, but when he caught her eye, the light tone in his voice turned serious.

"By the way, what happened with the truck?"

"We're hiking there tomorrow to see if it'll start," Troy said, his face glowing with excitement. "Wanna come?"

"We-ell ..." She glanced from father to son. "I don't have any boots."

"My dad's got a pair of old ones you could use."

Stella wrinkled her nose.

Troy giggled.

"Old but clean," Stan said.

"Too big," Stella said. "My feet 'll flip flop all over the place."

"We can stuff them," Troy said.

"Let me guess." She cast him a cursory glance. "Your dad's old socks."

Troy nodded. "The holey ones." He cracked up laughing.

"Are you game?" Stan asked, his words laced with meaning.

"Do I have a choice?"

"Always."

The one word came out a soft caress and triggered

a resurge of tender emotion inside her. Sheesh, just when she was getting her defenses in order, he had to slam dunk her with that.

"I wonder," she shot back, not wanting him to think her an easy mark.

"Don't," he said, tone serious.

A quiet moment passed, fraught with friction.

"By the way, there's been a change in the forecast. Rain this evening." Stan propped one arm on his knee. "Won't affect the snow up here because of the altitude, but should help clear the roads."

"Soon."

"Yes." Stan met and held her gaze. "Although black ice could be a hazard if temperatures dropped again."

"I'm a good skater." She attempted a joke, but it fell flat.

He chuckled, but it was a half-hearted sound.

Stella picked up a checker chip and flipped it in her palm to bridge the awkward moment.

"Can we still go hiking, Dad?"

"Sure thing, sport."

"I thought the snow was too deep to walk in safely." Stella dropped the chip on the table.

"Should be okay with snowshoes."

"I don't know how to snowshoe."

"It's easy, Sensei," Troy piped in. "I'll show you."

"Thank you, Troy. But I don't want to hold you up."

"You won't." Troy sorted the black and red checkers into two stacks.

"How far is it?"

"Thirty-minute trek," Stan said. "The truck's buried half in snow. I'd like to get it moving by tomorrow."

"Did it start, today?"

"Coughed and sputtered. After I dig it out, it should run okay."

"Then we can go to Vancouver," Troy exclaimed, plopping the checkers on the gameboard. "And see Stella's dojo."

After dinner, Stella took them both on and a couple of games later, Troy went to bed. While Stan tucked him in, Stella packed up the game and set it on the shelf.

"How 'bout a night cap?" Stan said, startling her.

He filled the doorway, and the warm spot surrounding her heart expanded, lighting her whole body. Emotion swelled ... *treading dangerous ground*, the warning sounded in her head.

"Sherry?" He strolled to the bar in the alcove by the window and filled a glass for her, and then poured himself a brandy.

She nodded, and bolted for the opposite end of the room.

"I won't pounce on you, you know." He fit the lid on the decanter and picked up the glasses.

"I'm sorry." Stella sat on the armchair by the blazing fire.

"Drink this." He reached over her shoulder and placed a glass in her hand, his fingers brushing hers. "It'll help you relax."

High voltage charged into her, and she gripped the glass in her palm. "I-I am relaxed."

He hiked a brow.

Stella tossed the drink back and it sizzled down her throat. "O-ooh," she gasped, slamming the glass on the table.

"Sip it slowly, savor the sweetness," he whispered, caressing her nape with his fingers.

"I should've." She scooted off the chair, swerved around so it was between them and clasped her hands by her sides. She'd spent the most intimate afternoon she'd ever had in her life with this man, yet felt jittery as a mouse stalked by a tiger. Ridiculous. Stan wasn't stalking her, he merely wanted to talk to her. *Get a grip, girl.*

"Another drink?" he invited, lounging on the sofa.

"No, thank you." She skirted around and plopped back on the chair. *Stop being so silly.* She folded her hands in her lap and waited.

Stan sipped his brandy and a deep crease crinkled his forehead. "This afternoon" –he paused, a hint of a smile on his lips— "this afternoon," he said again, and his smile vanished. "I came to ask for your help."

"With what?"

He shut his eyes and rubbed the bridge of his nose with his thumb. A beat, and he lifted his lashes, a storm brewing in his gaze. "With the custody battle." He rolled the brandy tumbler between his palms. "I spoke to my attorney and he ... uh ... suggested a quick way out of this mess."

"What're you going to do?"

He stared at the amber liquid in his glass for a long tense moment, then crushed her with his level gaze. "Get married."

Chapter 9

Stella's heart plummeted to her toes, his words like bullets lodging in her breast. She could hardly breathe. Dear God, what had she done? What had he? "How could y—"

"The lady is" —in one shot he downed his drink— "you."

Stella's heart flew up to heaven before it righted itself. A rush of oxygen filled her lungs. Goosebumps invaded her body from head to toe.

Stan stormed to the counter and refilled his glass, the amber liquid seeming to absorb all his attention.

"Me-e?" Air whooshed from her mouth, and she did a double take, staring him straight in the eye. "Why?"

"Because I want you, need—"

"Do you really, Rogers?" A pause, and Stella tilted her head. "Or could it be no one else's here to fit the bill for wife number two." She laughed, a brittle sound. "Or is it for sex?" Her heart kicked her chest, but the long years of discipline came to her aid and she didn't even blink.

Stan slammed the glass on the counter, liquid sloshing over the rim and splashing onto the glossy surface. "What went down this afternoon mean anything to you, Stella?"

"It meant a lot to me." Everything. But she didn't voice that shattering fact. "I wonder what it meant to you." She shot him a scathing glance. "A prelude for this evening's performance?"

"What's that supposed to mean?" In two strides he bridged the gap between them, flecks of ice in his eyes, his jaw jutting.

"You'd go to any length to keep your son, including—"

He pulled her from the chair so fast, she fell hard against his chest, her mouth nearly brushing his.

"Wouldn't you?" she accused.

"Yeah."

She slugged him in the chest and swept her foot across his ankle, knocking him off balance. He gripped her shoulders and dove onto the sofa with her beneath him.

"Oomph!" he grunted.

"Oomph!" she gasped.

"What you don't know is that I'd also go to any length to—"

"Snag what you want, fair or foul makes no difference

to you," Stella cut in, her contempt-riddled words grazing the already volatile atmosphere between them. Through the heat of her anger, she felt his hardness pressing into her, and desperately tried to ignore the sensations shooting into her. Her mind succeeded but her body craved ... and that fueled her anger. "And you want your son at any cost."

He filled his lungs with a rush of air, and then allowed breath to ease out between his lips. "Yes, I want my son." Wearily, he brushed a hand across his eyes. "Marriage is the simplest way to crack the legal maze."

"Start shopping." Her words snapped off her tongue like icicles. "I won't be used as a pawn for your deals."

"I'll make it worth your while."

Stella burst out laughing to avoid bursting into tears. She felt used. Yet it had seemed ... felt right ... with him. *Fool girl.*

He dropped the grenade. "The balance on your mortgage ... paid in full."

"I'm not for sale, Rogers." More games?

"When the price is right ..." A cynical twist to his mouth barred the rest of his words.

"No deal."

"I wouldn't be so hasty," he said. "That's five hundred thousand bucks you're tossing out the window."

She wished she could throw him out the window. "Some things don't carry a price tag." *Love for one,* the thought knifed through her. Now why had she thought that? Surely she wouldn't fall for that con ... yet the emptiness in her stomach and the battering of her heart sent another message. *Squash it.*

"No?"

She shoved him back, but he was like a brick wall not budging. "Get off me."

When he shifted, she wriggled from beneath him and leaped to her feet.

He sat up and plunked his head in his hands, his fingers scrubbing his scalp. A heavy beat, and he flung his head back, his eyes granite hard. "No deal ... no money ... no biz." He curled his lip, and the grenade exploded. "New owner."

Blood drained from her face. "You said you wouldn't—"

"I've changed my mind." His words unflinching.

"You have no interest in owning a Martial Arts dojo." She swallowed around the lump in her throat, her words crackling off her tongue.

"I do now." He stood, his jaw rigid. "You'd be smart to take the offer."

"You don't want a wife, Rogers" –she sucked in breath and let it burst from her lungs in force— "you want to buy me to play mother figure to gain custody of your son." Although her insides felt like mush gone sour, she stood firm.

"This is the only way I know to protect Troy."

He took a step closer.

She took a step back.

"Can you imagine what it'd do to him?" Another pace brought him close enough for him to cup her chin with his hand. "Do you?" He sighed, the sound detonating from deep inside him. "It'd destroy him."

It was destroying her.

"He'll crawl back into his shell, an insecure, lost little boy." His shoulders slumped. "I won't have my son go through hell again."

He'd have her go through it, instead. Her heart thumped. She could walk. Now. Couldn't she? This was not her problem ... yet it could turn into a dinosaur for her. Her mouth went dry. She didn't have to care ... she could find another lender, couldn't she? She licked her lips.

His eyes darkened.

Her gaze grew wary.

With one phone call, one e-mail he could hurl her back four years when she'd been knocking on his door with her empty pockets and a dream in her heart. She bent her head. The irony of it—he'd been the one to give her the chance to prove herself, and now, he was the one threatening to take it all away. Her dream ... her livelihood ... her future.

She was caught in the eye of the hurricane. Emotion flooded her being; an angry tear trickled down her cheek and splashed on his hand.

"I know this isn't the ideal proposal." He let go of her chin and wiped the wet streak on her face with his thumb.

His words sounded contrite, his touch tender, arousing—making her feel what she didn't want to ... for him. She had to remember he was a cunning businessman who would use, control and blackmail her ... to get what he wanted above all. His son.

The puzzle pieces fit.

Hadn't he seduced her mere hours ago? To set her up? And like a fool, she'd fallen like a ripe peach in his hand. She'd never slipped up before with any man ... keeping them at a distance. Yet with him she'd broken all her rules. She writhed with mortification. Every muscle in her body tensed, every nerve on alert ... she was about ready to strike back.

"It's a cold, calculating business proposition," she spat, erecting her shield. "Made by someone who has no heart."

She heard his sharp intake of breath and looked up. His face paled, the skin stretched taut across his cheekbones.

"You're very good at your trade, bag of tricks 'n all." She saw her advantage and took it, skewering him with a look of contempt. "Dangling a hefty contract before my eyes, thinking I'd snap it up."

A muscle battered his jaw. "When it's over, I'll release you, should you want to end it."

Stella wanted to scream. No. She loved him. No, she hated him. She pressed her fingers to her throbbing temples. She bit her lip, holding back the tears. She didn't know what she was feeling.

"I always think over my business ventures," she said, her voice stilted.

"Savvy move, Ryan."

Stella cast him a killing glance and marched to the door. With each step she took, she thought her legs would give out and she'd collapse in a heap on the floor. Her pulse bounced in her chest. Somehow, she had to outsmart him. Outmaneuver him. So when this was all over, Stan Rogers and his money couldn't touch her. But there'd be a price to pay for her freedom ... her heart.

"Stella."

At the sound of her name, her step faltered ... a split second of hesitation, and then she walked out, banging the door behind her. She crossed the hallway and slumped against the banister.

Her eyes welled up with tears. She heaved a wobbly breath and trudged up the stairs to her room, feeling no satisfaction that this time she'd left him standing with unanswered questions plaguing his mind.

Stella fell on the bed, raw pain ripping her insides

and sobs racking her body. Sniffing, she swiped the tears with the sheet, her eyes so puffy, she could hardly open them. Shivers shook her body. As much as she hated him, denied him, a little voice deep in her soul whispered she still loved him.

Eventually, the bout of weeping cut through tension coiled in her muscles, leaving her spent; yet oddly revived. She pushed her hair off her face, took several deep breaths and dragged herself from the bed. After undressing, she shuffled to the bathroom and splashed water on her face. Her skin tingled, but the gaping hole inside her chomped at her emotions. She blotted her cheeks dry with a towel and plodded back to bed, curling beneath the blankets.

Thoughts bombarded her brain.

Stella tossed and turned, the bed creaking beneath her. She pressed her knuckles to her mouth. What would her life be like without them? Her Martial Arts dojo ... provided she managed to hold onto it ... would keep her busy, but deep in her heart she knew it would never be the same.

Not now.

Not ever.

The man had rocked her world ... and she'd crashed. The boy, that little tike had gotten under her skin. She twisted her lips in a watery smile. Could she pick up the pieces ... take a chance on it? Could she do it for the boy alone? After all, Stan had been honest ... gave her his reasons for the marriage.

She shuddered, remembering his ways of persuasion. She deserved better. She punched the pillow, caught in an agony of indecision. The boy deserved better ... a business arrangement ... a bargain ... divorce ... it gave her a sick feeling in the pit of her stomach. She closed her eyes and her lids felt like lead. It was cold, calculating like Stan Rogers. She'd be a fool to even consider it.

*   *   *

After what seemed like moments, Stella awoke in a cold sweat, her head fuzzy and the hollow feeling gutting her insides. She whimpered.

Each word of his proposal cut into her memory like shards of ice. She huddled under the covers and peeked at the clock on the wall. Five a.m. She stole another moment in the warmth, then lugged herself from her cocoon, shivering.

Half an hour later, dressed in her jogging suit, an old sweater and mittens, Stella ventured out into early morning darkness. Snow glistened in the moonlight. She walked the trail around the lodge and snow crystals crackled beneath her sneakers.

An icy blast smacked her face, stinging her cheeks.

She breathed the fresh crispness of dawn and exhaled, her breath frosting in the air. She slapped her mittened hands together for warmth and glanced up. The trees stood like silent protectors around her, and far above them, a star twinkled despite the approaching daylight. She felt ephemeral somehow, like being a part of another time, another place, another planet.

The serenity of the forest was a contrast to her turbulent feelings, and helped her bring things into perspective. She still had a choice. Final decision was hers. She whispered a quick prayer up to heaven, and in that moment in time, she knew what she had to do. With a determined step in her stride, she made her way to the gym.

Stella flung off the heavy sweater and mittens, and ran the track like her life depended on it. It did. Perspiration oozed from her every pore, her heart rate racing. At last, she slowed to a trot, then a walk, cooling down.

"Got it out of your system?" Stan's edgy words made her jump.

"Must you sneak up on me?" She whirled around, clashing with the steel of his eyes.

"Was not."

"Were too."

An uncertain smile happened between them, then, uncomfortable silence bumped by for several seconds.

Dressed in jeans and a white sweater, he leaned against a pillar, feet bare, arms folded across his chest. His hair was still damp from his recent swim. The sight of him took her breath away. She had no right to feel like that; not after what he'd done to her.

Seduced her. Used her.

Taken her virginity.

Naa, the voice niggled her brain. You gave, my girl … you were a willing participant.

She swallowed and then bristled. How dare he stand there as if he hadn't a care in the world.

"What're you doing here?" she asked, curtly.

"Same as you." His eyes never left her face. "Couldn't sleep."

"Oh."

"Watch yourself in the water, Ryan."

"I'm capable of taking care of myself."

His gaze probed, deepened. "I wonder." He sauntered to the door and tossed over his shoulder, "See you at breakfast."

Stella dove into the pool, weaving through the water, each lap cooling her fury.

Purposely, she delayed her appearance for breakfast and breathed a sigh of relief at the vacant table. It was a short reprieve. Soon after, they snow-shoed through the forest to the Hummer, Minni and the guys had abandoned for the limo ride into town.

141

While Stan tinkered under the hood, Stella ducked Troy's snow missiles but still got the worst of it. She swerved away from his next shot, and the snowball smacked his dad on the back of the head.

"Oops," Troy giggled.

Stella chuckled.

Stan growled. Scooping up handfuls of snow, he bombarded them both; Troy's squeals of delight echoed through the forest glen.

"Enough." Stan wiped his hands dry on his jacket and turned his attention back to the engine. "I've almost got this baby working." Another snowball hit him between the shoulder blades and he whipped around, targeting Stella with his cool gaze. "You're playing dirty, ma'am."

She elevated both eyebrows.

He dismissed the nick to his conscience. "I wasn't looking."

"It wasn't me." She backed away from him, lost her footing and tumbled onto a snowbank, the white fluff like cotton candy around her.

He stomped for her.

She held her arms up to ward him off.

He pounced, held her down with his body and washed her face with a handful of snow. Spluttering, she tried to explain, but he took no notice.

"Get off me, Rogers." She shoved him back, a smile

plastered to her face for the boy's sake; inside she felt frost-bitten.

His eyes glinted hard. "Sure thing." He pushed himself off her, turned a stiff back and resumed fiddling with the engine.

Stella scrambled up and shook snow off her hair and body. Troy laughed when it sprayed on him.

"Come here, you little minx." She scooped a handful of snow and chased after him.

"Na, nana, nana." Troy took cover behind his father, shaped another missile and fired at her.

The battle raged on.

Stella toppled onto another snowdrift, the dampness seeping through her clothes and chilling her flesh. "Time out." She leapt up, grabbed the backpack beneath a Douglas fir and took out the thermos ... her bargaining chip. "You want hot chocolate, put your ammo down." She winked.

Troy gulped his drink and munching on a chocolate chip cookie, rolled snow into a giant ball. Stan declined the snack with a grunt and a shake of his head, his hair ruffling in the breeze. A twinge of emotion poked her heart, but she squashed it. Quickly, she replaced the thermos in the backpack and helped Troy build his snowman. Keeping busy helped.

About mid afternoon, Stan dusted his hands off, slipped his gloves on and signaled the return to the lodge. Troy traipsed after him and Stella brought up the rear, feeling Stan's overpowering presence even in the great outdoors. Sexual awareness teased her nerves like an electrical current, and she kept her distance.

When the lodge came in sight, Stan called a halt by the garage and removed his snowshoes. After he helped Troy with his, he glanced at her. "Need help with yours?"

"No."

"Fine."

Of course with him watching, she became all thumbs, and gritting her teeth, determined not to ask for his help. At last, she slipped the snowshoes off and held them out to him. He grabbed the pair from her hands and marched into the garage, without a word, without a backward glance.

Troy skipped ahead of her into the house and made a beeline for the kitchen. Stella went upstairs. A change of clothes would chase the chill from her bones, but wouldn't do much for the frost encircling her heart. A cup of hot tea might help though.

By the time she walked back downstairs to the kitchen, Stan had cloistered himself in his office and Troy was swallowing the last of the chocolate from the thermos. She hid a smile. A chocolaty mustache outlined his upper lip, a sprinkle of cookie crumbs on his chin.

"Video game or lesson?" She motioned to a napkin on the table.

"Bonzai!" Troy leaped from his chair, his hands in a Karate chop and swooped up the napkin to wipe his mouth.

Stella chuckled all the way to the gym, and the tightening around her heart loosened ... just a tad.

Later that evening, after Troy had gone to bed, she stacked the dishwasher, and feeling restless, strolled to the library. The warmth of the room soothed. She plopped down on the sofa, deep in thought and stared at the flames in the hearth.

"Good, you're still here." Stan marched inside, his words breaking into her reverie.

Stella leaped up and skirted past him to the door.

"Just a minute." He caught her elbow and halted her exit. "An answer."

Stella twisted from his grasp, her eyes warring with this. "Yes." The word snapped off her tongue like an icicle. "For the child."

"Of course, Troy." Stan seemed to pale, but the hard edge in his voice belied that. "We'll be married in three days."

"So-o soon?" she whispered. "What if the roads don't clear?"

"They should." He nodded. "If not, I'll radio for the chopper."

"Chopper?" Something clicked in her brain and she stared at him, aghast. "We were never stuck up here?

There was always a way out?"

"Of course," he replied reasonably. "The helicopter was a call away in case of an emergency."

"Why didn't you tell me?"

"You decided to stay." He squinted at her. "The subject didn't arise afterward."

"I could've been home days ago." She fisted her hands and paced the floor. If she had, she wouldn't be in this predicament ... wouldn't be feeling ... "Minni and the guys could've been back by now?"

"Yes and yes." He cast her a candid look. "But since the choppers were in short supply the first week of the blizzard, the group decided to visit family in the city. A much deserved break."

"You manipulating—" Stella bit off the epithet, shaking her head. "You're going to pay—"

"How much," he goaded, taking out his checkbook. "The title deed worth five-hundred grand not enough for you?"

"Not about money," she flared at him. "No amount of coin is going to change what you did."

"You're going back on your word then?" he challenged.

She stood like an ice maiden, and even her close proximity to the fire didn't thaw her.

"You're misunderstanding me," he said, a hint of impatience in his voice.

"No, I'm not," she fired back. "You're the one who doesn't get it." A sigh sounded from deep inside her, a mixture of frustration and sadness.

"I'm not backing on my word," she murmured so quietly, he strained to hear. "But I am making an amendment to the agreement."

He tilted his head, his eyes slitted, every muscle in his body seeming to coil. The lion was prepping for battle ... with her.

She tried to speak, but her voice cracked. She filled her lungs with oxygen, exhaled in force and straightened to her full five foot six inches. She placed her hands on her hips, her gaze level with his. "This mockery of a marriage will be a business deal," she said, voice devoid of emotion. "You'll be husband in name only and you'll keep your hands off me."

"Catch?" The muscles in his neck grew rigid, his eyes hard.

She curved her lips, not quite a smile. He was astute enough to know she had him cornered.

"You'll pay off the balance of the note, as you ... uh ... so generously offered, and hand over the title deed to my dojo with me named sole owner." Stella cringed, her stomach churning, her palms moist. She felt like a mercenary.

She had to be tough ... hard ... smart.

"And another five hundred thousand cash." A gold

digger couldn't be much worse. But she had to be sure he didn't come after her assets, and if he did, she wanted to bank enough capital to bail herself out. "Delivered on the wedding date."

He laughed, a hollow sound, lifeless. "Dangling a price tag, Stella?"

"I changed my mind." She threw back his words of moments ago.

"After you have custody of the child, I'll sue for divorce, in a timely fashion to least affect Troy."

He paled, the skin taut across his cheekbones, his eyes narrowed.

"I'd suggest you consider my offer," she said, her words brittle. "With your net worth, Mr. R, you're getting a bargain."

Stan tightened his jaw, his nostrils flaring. "Since I'll be getting a bride for a bargain" –he swept his gaze over her, pausing at her cleavage, then lower to skim the apex of her thighs, and finally shooting back to the ice storm in her eyes— "I'll be sure to make the most of my ... uh ... good fortune."

"And I mine." She gave him the once over, matching his insolent look, but a tremor shook her.

Dare she believe he'd keep his end of the bargain? He wielded deals in his best interests or those he cared for. She didn't fall into that category. He'd use every tactic at his disposal, including her, to win the prize.

His son.

Could she match him at his ruthless game?

A dangerous silence crackled between them.

Shivers shimmied up her spine, and she rubbed her arms with her hands, wondering if he could read her thoughts.

"If you've quite finished your analysis," he said, his voice vibrating with controlled menace. "I suggest you go get ready for your wedding day."

His words shot into her like pellets. She raised a hand to slap his face, he intercepted it in mid-air and yanked her hard against his chest. A blue blizzard raged in his eyes. His mouth inches from hers, his breath grazing her lips.

She shivered and licked her lips.

His hands steeled on her shoulders, a growl low in his throat.

An explosive moment hung between them.

"Go." He released her so suddenly, she stumbled back a step. "Before I change my mind and sample my bargain bride." His brazen gaze hot on her body, his savage words hitting too hard and fast for her to deflect.

Stella twisted away, her head held high and bit the quiver from her bottom lip.

The woman got to him, big time. Stan fueled his lungs with oxygen, took a step to make amends, then halted. *Not a good idea right now, buster.*

She marched to the door, grabbed the knob for support and shot him a blistering glance over her shoulder. "I've learned to make the most of my bargains, too, Rogers." She shoved the door open, stepped out and slammed it shut it behind her.

"From me, no doubt," Stan muttered, striding to the bar. He poured himself a stiff drink and in one gulp downed it, welcoming the burning heat in his throat. The smell of liquor tantalized, he reached for the open brandy bottle. A tense pause, and he hurled his empty glass into the fireplace, smashing it into a million pieces. Drowning his sorrows in a bottle of booze was not the answer...

It hadn't worked before when he'd come home half plastered over a mega deal gone belly up and found his ex strung out and sprawled on his bed. She'd given him some sob story, and like a callow college youth of twenty, he'd believed she wanted a reconciliation.

In the morning, nursing a doozer of a hangover, he stumbled from the bed, only to find she'd hit the road together with his cash and credit cards.

A nightmare revisited.

She'd left him nothing more than a note scribbled with, 'Thanks for the tip ... and the night darling.'

As it turned out, that hadn't been all ... Troy had been the result of that ill-fated night.

Breath constricted in his chest at the thought of his son.

He should have booted her out from the start, but unlike his parents, he wanted to make the marriage work. When he was five, his parents had divorced and he'd been shuffled from relative to relative. At eighteen, he'd tripped out on his own and soon after bumped into Ann. On a reckless dare he married her, and once again everything in his life spiraled out of control.

Castigating himself for being dumped a second time, he'd vowed off women and concentrated on building his business to mega proportions. He'd picked up the high risk loan accounts nobody wanted, and in a few years he'd become a force to reckon with in the global financial playing field.

A growl built in his throat. It had worked.

Until Sensei here showed up at his office four years ago ... and made him feel again. That had signaled danger to his controlled lifestyle and so, he'd quickly shipped her off to one of his associates to close the deal on her dojo.

But he'd kept her in the back of his mind, under lock and key, until Troy landed on his doorstep. And then, he had to confront her and his demons.

Every woman is not Ann, the voice in his head insisted. *Oh yeah?!* Wasn't Stella setting him up by upping the ante to take him for all he was worth?

Could any woman be trusted?

A muscle boxed his jaw.

Was history repeating itself?

In a heavy mood, Stan stalked from the library and grabbed his coat off the rack in the hallway. He flung open the door, stepped outside and yanked it shut behind him. He walked the grounds; the icy layer of snow grinding beneath his boots, the only sound invading the quiet of nature.

That's not how he'd meant it to be with this woman. He hoped, no, prayed Stella would understand. A raw sound exploded from him. When had anyone ever tried to understand, be on his side? All had been after what they could get out of him.

He booted pebbles in his path onto the snowbank.

When he was a kid collecting soda cans for pennies, his 'friends' were after him for loans. When a gangly teenager, he was followed for what he could deliver intellectually to his classmates. As an adult, women flocked to him for his pocketbook. What made him think Stella would be any different? Hadn't she agreed to marry him to reap a crafty worded contract and pocket a cool mil?

I'll do it for the boy. Her words echoed in his brain, and savagely, he shoved them aside. She was hooking him for what she could get— an ace of a one-sided prenup. He'd be smart to remember that.

* * *

Three days later Stella married the ogre in a small, quiet wedding at the registrar's office. The guests were Minni, Joe and Fred. Troy, his face alight with excitement, stood next to his father. Stella breathed a sigh of relief; her concern about his reaction had been unfounded.

Not wanting any of her friends to witness this farce of a marriage, she'd kept "mum" about it; except for a quick call to Toronto to tell her parents the news. Her mother had been ecstatic and her two brothers already married with children had whooped it up. The impossible had happened. Stella was getting married.

A whimsical smile brushed her lips. Her father had always told her the man she chose to marry would be worth the wait. Her mouth drooped, and then she forced it back into a semblance of a smile for appearances. What they didn't know and wouldn't know, were the conditions of the marriage.

Several hours before the wedding, Stella had returned to her studio with Minni lending motherly support. She dressed in a creme-colored dress with an off-the shoulder neckline trimmed with lace that had hung in her closet for ages, sales tag and all. Since most social events she attended revolved around Martial Arts, she'd had little use for it.

She couldn't very well get married in a Karate gui, now, could she? A moment of thought, then a grin feathered her lips. And why not?

Her smile dipped. She'd worked too hard to establish herself as a Martial Artist; her gui and black belt signified solid achievement. Keeping her business afloat, made her determined to go through with this travesty. And to retain her sanity, she had to keep work separate from the marriage ... had to feel she had her independence.

She wore the sheerest of silk stockings and white, high-heeled pumps. She left her hair loose and it fell like a soft wave about her shoulders.

Just before they left, Minni pushed a bouquet of pink roses into her hands. "Oh, Missy." Minni had fussed around her like a mother hen. "Mr. Rogers' not going to know what hit him."

It was winter but Stella looked like spring. If only she felt as bright and cheerful, she thought, forcing a smile but it belied the sadness in her soul.

*   *   *

All too soon, Fred swerved the limo to a stop in front of the downtown building. Butterflies the size of torpedoes bombarded her stomach, and Stella prayed she got through the ordeal. Joe helped her from the car and she clutched his proffered arm like a lifeline. Grinning, he patted her gloved hand and escorted her up the stairs and through the glass doors. Fred and Minni followed close behind. Joe walked her to her future husband's side, and her step faltered only once.

Unsmiling, Stan stood waiting for her. The white shirt and tie he wore beneath a navy suit did nothing to diminish the distance between them. Yet she was so close to him, his heat brushed her skin, the fresh outdoor scent of his aftershave enveloped her. A blink of his lashes, and he quenched the glint that had lit his eyes upon her approach.

Stella gulped down the hysterical sound rising in her throat. Since all he'd seen her in were oversized clothes and shabby sneakers, she must've caught him by surprise dressed in feminine clothes. That or a trick of the light, she reasoned, choking the bouquet between her hands.

When Stan slipped the ring on her finger, she trembled. His touch pierced her frozen shield, his heat charging through her and cracking the ice around her heart. The double ring ceremony had puzzled her, and she'd glanced at him in surprise. He arched an eyebrow, daring her to question it. Then he kissed her, the merest brush of his mouth upon hers, but his hands on her shoulders held her steady. When he stepped away, his eyes held hers for a timeless moment.

Stella blinked the connection away. She was a mass of nerves but no one seemed to notice, seeming to credit her pale face and Stan's grim look to wedding day jitters.

Finally, the ordeal was over. Stan took her elbow and

guided her outside to flashing cameras and showers of confetti.

Troy reached up to kiss her cheek and she hugged him. In a grown-up manner, he turned to his father and shook his hand.

"Throw the bouquet," someone called.

Shaken from her bemused state, Stella threw the spray of roses over her shoulder. At the howls of laughter, she spun around and joined in. Fred held the flowers in his hands, a sheepish grin on his face.

Soon after, the wedding party celebrated with a champagne lunch at one of Vancouver's star seaside hotels, The Westin Bayshore Inn. Stella barely swallowed a mouthful of the steak and lobster on her plate. Stan too, ate very little. Troy, however, wolfed down his food with youthful gusto.

Mock marriage, mock honeymoon, Stella thought feeling a little lightheaded ... and she'd only had one glass of champagne. She waved good-bye to everyone and reluctantly grasped Stan's outstretched hand. A jolt shot through her, and she stumbled in her step.

"Steady." Stan gripped her hand tighter and helped her into the front seat of the limo. Troy clambered in back and he slid into the driver's seat.

After ensuring they were buckled in, he pulled out into the late afternoon traffic on Georgia Street. To an onlooker they must seem the happy family ... an anguished sound gurgled in her throat.

"Something wrong?" Stan asked, tone impersonal. He drove by Stanley Park and onto Lion's Gate Bridge that would get them into North Vancouver and on the road back to the mountain lodge.

Stella shook her head, not trusting herself to speak. She wouldn't cry. Not in front of him and the child. Later, in the privacy of her room, she could let loose and sob her heart out. What had she done? She would have to come to terms with the chaos of her life. But one decision she'd already made. Within days she planned to re-open her studio.

Snowdrifts bordered the road, but the driveway to the lodge was clear. The moment Stan turned into it and ground to a halt, Stella jumped from the vehicle. She was ready to barge through the front door but the 'Newly Married' sign decorated with pine boughs, gave her pause.

"Oh my." Mistiness pressed against her lashes at Minni's and the guys' handiwork.

"Thoughtful," Stan uttered, unlocking the front door.

"Dad, you're supposed to carry my Sensei mom," Troy blurted, fidgeting beside him, "over the threshold and kiss her."

Stella signaled no to Stan with a covert gaze. He, on the other hand, clasped his son on the shoulder and tilted the corner of his mouth in a smile.

"Sounds like a good idea, m' boy." He winked at Troy and scooped her up in his arms.

The moment he touched her, awareness ripped through her and she wriggled in his hold.

"The boy," Stan whispered in her ear.

She opened her mouth to toss him a spicy retort, and he planted a kiss on her parted lips, crossing the threshold.

"Welcome home, Mrs. Rogers," he whispered, searching deep in her eyes.

"Put me down," she mouthed, while Troy closed the door behind him.

"Sure thing, Mrs. Rogers," he mouthed right back, setting her on her feet none too gently.

"Don't call me that." She scampered away, his chuckle following her up the stairs and chilling her hot skin.

* * *

The rest of the day seemed no different from any other. Stan sequestered himself in his study and worked on his accounts. Stella changed into her gui and gave Troy his Karate lesson.

As daylight waned into evening twilight, Troy helped her serve a cozy dinner by the fireside on paper plates. The plates would be fuel for the fire. Was there a hidden meaning in that? She was already in hot water with the ogre with this sham of a wedding. Said ogre was now setting two crystal goblets filled with champagne on the table, the exception to the paper dining decor. But he'd insisted. She'd shrugged, refusing to be drawn into another argument with him. He handed a glass of milk to Troy and one with the bubbly to her.

"May this marriage risk all." Stan raised his glass, his gaze level with hers.

His words befuddled her brain, but she took a sip, the fizz tickling her nose.

Troy lifted his glass, flicked a champagne drop sliding down the bottle's neck and licked it off his finger. "Yech!" He made a face.

Stella laughed.

"Enough of that young man," Stan scolded, but his mouth twitched at the corners. "Go brush your teeth and get to bed. I'll be up in a minute."

Troy set his glass on the table and jumped up. "Wou ... ould it be okay if my new mom came too?"

Stan raised a brow at her.

"Of course," she said. "I'll zip up as soon as you're ready." She tilted her lips in a secret smile. "I'll tell you a funny story about a karate kid."

"Oh, wow!" Troy took a step toward her, but shyness overtook him and he turned away. Seconds later, he hurled back, hugging his father, then Stella. Just as quickly, he dashed out and up the stairs.

"Nice to know he's happy," Stan murmured.

"Yes." Stella nodded and collected the dishes.

"Leave them," he said. "Tomorrow 'll be soon enough to begin your wifely duties."

"What's that supposed to mean?"

"Exactly like it sounds."

"If you think that I ... you ... again," she fumbled with words. "You're greatly mistaken."

"Are you inviting me into your bed, Mrs. Rogers?"

Stella glared at him. "I don't repeat my mistakes, Rogers."

"That makes two of us." He glared back at her.

"You're impossible." She leaped up and marched to the door.

He shrugged, following her up the stairs to Troy's room but the child was already asleep.

"Must've been exhausted." He turned to her. "It's been a long day for you, too, hasn't it?"

Stella kissed the child's brow and adjusted the blankets around him.

"Cut out the pretense," she murmured, heading for the door. "He's asleep."

"But you're not." He glanced at his son and followed her from the room. "You look worn out. You'd better get to bed.

"Thanks for the thought," she said, voice dripping with sarcasm. "That's my intention, going to bed."

"Good," he replied. "I'm going to have another look around, lock up and come up and join you."

Chapter 10

"What?" Stella spun on him. "That wasn't part of the bargain."

"But this was." He tossed an envelope into her hands and sauntered past her downstairs.

She stood transfixed to the spot. The envelope burned her fingers, and she wanted to hurl it back in his face, but it wasn't quite the time. She pocketed it in case she needed a "bargaining chip". She shut her eyes tight, her heart thudding, her palms moist.

Patience ... not one of her virtues.

Just then, she heard him bounding back up the stairs and her eyes flew open, her pulse leaping. She slipped inside her room, shut the door and leaned her head against it. He walked past, but was there a pause in his stride in front of her door or was it her imagination? When she heard his bedroom door open and shut, she breathed a sigh of relief. She flicked on the light switch, blinked at the sudden brightness and turned around.

She gasped. She gaped.

The bed was stripped, the closet empty and her luggage missing. She yanked the door open, marched down the hall and banged on his door.

"Easy there, Mrs. Rogers." He opened his bedroom door and leaned against the jamb, his arms folded across his chest. "We've got all night." He winked.

Stella opened her mouth to spit a retort, but he caught her wrist, pulling her against his chest. His eyes shackled hers. A tremor ran through her. He swooped down and took her lips in a kiss that shook her equilibrium all the way to her toes.

He lifted his head and brushed her mouth with his thumb. "You were about to say something?"

She knocked his hand away and pressed her fingers to her mouth. Before she could hurl a mouthful of verbal bullets his way, he lifted her into his arms, kicked the bedroom door shut and tossed her on the bed.

"I will not sleep with you, Rogers." She scrambled off the bed, breath bursting from her mouth. "Where's my luggage? I want to go to my room."

He inclined his head toward the closet, and she rushed over, flinging the panels open. Her clothes hung neatly beside his.

"Considerate of Minni, don't you think?" he said, ever so quietly.

Not bothering to answer, Stella grabbed her two suitcases, threw them open at her feet and tossed her clothes inside. "I have no intention of spending the night with you, now or ever."

"Never is a long time." He shifted, standing between her and the door. "Just where do you think you're going?"

"Back to my own bedroom," she snapped. "This wasn't part of the deal." She picked up a suitcase and shoved past him. "I'll be back for the other one."

"I'll get it for—"

"No, thank—" She spun around and the case in her hands bumped the one in his and it slipped from her fingers, crashing to the floor.

"Now look at what you've done." She glared at him, then at her clothes strewn across the floor.

"Me?" He chuckled, setting the case he held down.

"Must you resort to boardroom tactics when you don't get your own way?" she flared, tempted to stomp her foot.

His chuckle dissolved into silence. Ominous quiet.

"I'll not stay here with you."

"So you said." His gaze shadowed.

She stooped down and gathered her clothes. "I'll be on my way."

"I think not."

Her head snapped up and she leaped up, hugging the bundle to her bosom. "You can think what you want, but I'll—"

"We will share a bed tonight and every night."

"I will not."

"Then you may use the floor."

"I will not."

"You choose. Bed or floor," he said unflinchingly. "But in this room you will spend your nights with me."

"I will not!"

"You will, Mrs. Rogers," Stan said in a voice that brooked no argument. "I will not have my son and my staff wondering why we're sleeping in separate bedrooms." He paused, his eyes blue ice in a face of stone. "We will make this appear a normal, happy marriage."

Her heart hurt and her head ached. Had she made the biggest mistake of her life in agreeing to this charade of a marriage? But for the boy's sake, she had to try.

"I'll share the room with you, Rogers, but nothing more." She dumped her clothes in the open suitcase, thinking the Arctic Ice Cap couldn't be half as frozen as she felt.

"As you wish." He swept up a transparent silk and lace undergarment and handed it to her.

"What do you think you're doing?" She grabbed the flimsy garment from his hands.

"Helping."

"Don't."

"Sure thing, Mrs."

She turned with a ready retort, but he'd already moved to the bed and stripped off his shirt. A jolt charged through her. She averted her eyes and sorted through her clothes, her hands trembling. If she didn't guard against the potency of his sexuality, the fire flaring between them could annihilate her.

"You may have the bathroom first," he let fly over his shoulder.

"Thank you, you go." *Yes, go, leave the room so I can breathe.*

When she heard the shower running, her imagination ran rampant ... water sluicing down his bronzed body, plastering hair on his chest and lower to— She collapsed on the settee, picked up a brush from the dresser and yanked it through her hair over and over. The shiny waves flowed about her shoulders. By the time he came out, she felt like her scalp had been injected with a thousand pins and needles.

"All yours, Mrs. Rogers." He ambled by and the scent of fresh soap wafted to her. Barefoot and dressed only in pajama bottoms, he tossed back the covers and got into bed.

Her stomach fluttered and her breath pocketed in her chest.

Stella collected her night things and shut herself in the bathroom. She took her sweet time showering, brushing her teeth and dressing. By the time she opened the door a crack and peered out, he'd turned out the lights. A moonbeam streamed through the window and illuminated her way.

She tiptoed to the bed and stared at her sleeping husband, her white nightie swirling around her feet. Chill in the air turned her skin to gooseflesh and she rubbed her hands over her arms. She bit her lip, debating between the floor and the bed.

"Come to bed, Stella," he mumbled, startling her. Without turning her way, he threw back the blankets on her side. "It's much warmer."

Stella glared at his rigid back, then at the bed and finally at the floor, hard and cool beneath her feet. She curled her toes, thinking it'd be silly to stand there and catch a cold. Gingerly, she slipped into bed and pulled the blankets over her, lying as far away from him as possible.

"Relax, I won't bite." Stan shifted to a more comfortable position and the bed squeaked. "At least not tonight."

She drew in a sharp breath and remained immobile, afraid to move lest she touch him.

"Goodnight," he muttered.

"Goodnight," she murmured.

A tremulous sigh escaped her lips, and unclenching her hands, she turned her face to the wall. Tears, silent as her pain slipped beneath her lashes and down her cheeks.

Next morning, sunlight filtering through the crack in the curtains, teased Stella awake. She squinted at the brightness, then stiffened, remembering whose bed she shared. Slowly, she turned her head, saw the dent in the pillow and relaxed. She twitched her nose, and every cell in her body buzzed. His scent emanated from the rumpled sheets, a strong reminder of the man who'd slept beside her.

She drew the covers up to her chin and surveyed the room. It was sparsely furnished, the walnut chest of drawers matched the bed's headboard in design and the carpet in color. Simple, direct and to the point, like the owner. The dresser and mirror, the only feminine touch in a very masculine room must've been brought for her. His consideration for her comforts touched a soft spot in her heart, then she nearly snorted. More like a bribe, she thought, recalling what had recently transpired between them. She steeled her nerves and got out of bed. No matter the reasons, there would be repercussions regarding her marriage to Stan.

Thirty minutes later, Stella descended the stairs to a deserted kitchen smelling of burnt toast and coffee. Troy was still asleep, but a mug and dish on the drainboard cued that Stan had been and gone. She dropped a bread slice in the toaster, took the carton of orange juice from the refrigerator and poured a glass.

Stella sipped the drink and contemplated the outdoors through the window above the sink. A second later, the toast popped up and picking it up, she nibbled the crust. Thoughts clamored in her brain ... in less than two weeks her world had turned topsy-turvy ... and she didn't know how to right it. She downed the drink and set the glass in the sink with force.

The hours crawled by. Stella went through her exercise routine, and after giving Troy his lesson, fixed a quick meal for them. Stan had a sandwich in his study. Dinner was not much different.

When it was time to tackle the bedroom demarcation, she made sure she was in bed and 'sleeping' before he came in. He must've had similar thoughts for he didn't venture up until after midnight ... and that suited her fine, right?

On Monday morning, Stella bundled Troy in warm clothes, boosted him up into the Hummer and climbed in beside him. A few minutes later, Stan leaped into the driver's seat and fastened his seatbelt.

"Ready?" he said, inserting the key in the ignition.

She nodded.

"Oh, boy!" Troy watched his father back the truck out and drive along the trail to the main road.

Stan smiled at his son's jubilation, but said very little during the drive.

Stella watched snow-drenched pines whizzing by, trying to ignore his silence and the rigid set of his jaw.

"I'm really going to see your Karate studio, Mom ... uh ... Sensei," Troy asked, his excited chatter easing tension in the confines of the vehicle.

"Of course." Stella patted his arm with affection. "You'll be working out there from now on."

"That'll depend how often we come into Van." Stan glanced her way and the groove on his forehead deepened.

"I hope it's lots." Troy bounced on the seat between them.

Stella grinned, pleased.

Stan grunted, a non-committal reply.

Two hours later, he pulled up in front of the studio and just as soon as Stella climbed out, Troy jumped into her arms.

"See you at one for lunch." Stan didn't miss his son holding her hand, and the grim set of his mouth intensified. His eyes locked on hers, and about to say something more, he changed his mind and drove off.

Stella watched until the truck's taillights disappeared around the corner and a deep sigh blew from her lips.

"Come on, kid." She pulled the starry-eyed Troy with her up the two steps to the dojo. "We're on major clean-up duty." She flung the windows open to get rid of the musty smell, picked up two dusters and tossed one to him. "You gotta work for your keep, m' boy. Now, get to it."

When they were done, Stella took a packet from the cabinet, and smiling, she handed it to him. "An early Christmas present."

Troy tore off the wrapping. "Oh, wow!" He touched the Karate gui with reverence and tied the white belt around his waist.

"Come on." Stella smiled and motioned for him to go through the curtained partition to the training floor for his first lesson in the dojo.

He gaped at the Championship trophies lined up against one wall, then made a beeline for the heavy bag hanging from the wooden beam on the ceiling. He punched and kicked, but the bag refused to budge. "Ouch!" He rubbed his fist and flexed his leg.

"Easy, there." Stella got in position and landed a roundhouse kick onto the bag, the impact swinging it back and forth. "Using the punch bag will strengthen your arm and leg muscles and perfect your technique." She caught the bag to steady it. "Now, you try."

While he practiced, Stella attacked the stacks of mail and fielded calls from her friends and students.

"Keia," Troy yelled, smacking the bag with a front kick.

She smiled. "There you go, you're doing it."

"How's the lesson going, young karateka?" Stan called

from the doorway, his sudden reappearance, causing prickles to shimmy up her spine.

"Oh, Dad, you shoulda seen me smash that bag!" Troy ran to his father and showed off his new gui.

"Nice." Stan chuckled.

"It was so much fun!" Troy said, bopping up and down.

"Sensei's doing a good job, eh?" Stan patted his son's shoulder, his eyes seeking and holding Stella's own. "Hungry?"

Troy nodded. Stella didn't.

As soon as Troy dashed out to change, the air grew thick. Stella's nerves stretched to breaking point, a defense against the emotional undertow between them.

"Impressive," Stan said, catching sight of the trophies.

His tone was so casual, it had her stiffening with indignation. She was so wound up, nearly palpitating at his close proximity, and him seeming to be on neutral.

"Thank you," she said, voice stilted, polite. "Not all mine. Some belong to my students."

"Come now, you're too modest." He stood with legs apart and arms folded across his broad chest, gazing down at her. "And if I remember correctly" – he paused for effect— "you don't like to dine in a gui."

"I'm ... uh ... not very hungry."

His eyes slitted. "After that dry toast this morning, I figured you might be."

"How'd ..." she began. "You were nowhere about."

He brushed his bearded chin with the back of his hand. "Wasn't I?"

She grilled him with her gaze, and when he didn't turn away, she blinked, rifling through the papers on her desk.

"You were staring out the kitchen window, miles away."

"I see."

"Do you, Stella?"

"Is that supposed to mean something?" she asked.

A steady look, then he shrugged. "Sure about lunch?"

"I've got to catch up on work." A silent moment passed ... a loaded moment, her pulse kicked her rib, and she had to ask. "How was your meeting this morning?"

"As expected."

"That doesn't tell me much," she said, the air pocket in her throat breaking free with her words.

"Not much to say." He set his mouth.

"Stan ..."

"They're deliberating over testimony, Stella." He shoved a tuft of hair off his brow, the motion a reflection of the stress he was under. "Next week, you and I have a session with them."

About to fire more questions at him, she curbed her tongue when Troy bounded back. She'd expected to be called in as witness, but not so soon.

"You wanna a hotdog, Mom?" Troy asked, cooling the friction between them. "We could bring one back for you."

Stella smiled. "Thanks, but I'm not very hungry." She winked. "Since you had an extra long work out, you can have mine."

"Bonzai!" Troy raised his fist in a victory signal.

"We'll pick you up around four." Stan ushered Troy out the door.

"That should give you plenty of time to pull yourself together." He allowed his gaze to travel over her slender figure wrapped loosely in her Karate gui, black belt hanging from her hips. He glanced down at her bare feet, then up to the moist sheen on her face; damp tendrils loose from her ponytail clung to her nape and temples. If it wasn't for the child nearby, he'd—the woman had him clenching his gut, searing his lower extremities, his vitals skyrocketing.

"But first" –he reached out and pulled her closer— "a good-bye kiss."

He'd barely brushed her mouth, when he let her go and hobbled back a step in utter consternation. She'd just landed her heel crisply on his foot.

"When will you stop fighting me, spitfire?" He snagged her arm and hauled her up so close he could see the violet flecks in her eyes.

"S'long, darling." She smiled sweetly and twisted away. A challenge. Definitely.

"Later," he growled.

*   *   *

The sun had sunk behind the mountains, turning the sky crimson gold by the time Stan swerved to a stop in front of the lodge. Stella hopped from the truck and stumbled through the front door, wanting nothing more than to soak in a warm bath. Troy and Stan followed close behind. But since she'd missed lunch, the smell wafting from the kitchen lured her in that direction.

Minni bustled out, wiping her hands on her apron. "Welcome aboard, dear," she said, a twinkle in her eye.

Joe and Fred smiled at her and shook hands with Stan.

"Thank you," Stella and Stan replied simultaneously.

Minni cooked a delicious meal of baked salmon, rice pilaf with herbs and vegetables almondine. The bottle of Chardonnay gracing the table, complimented the fare with just the right touch of magic. Although Minni and the two men usually dined in their own quarters, tonight, since it was their first day back, they joined the family, making it a party. Stella enjoyed their jovial teasing and good-natured fun, wondering how she could've thought these two, sweet men were hoods wanting to harm her.

"Mmm ... thanks loads, Minni," Troy mumbled, wiping chocolate crumbs from his lips. "That was real good."

"Thank ye, lad."

After the staff left, Stan shut himself in his study and Stella and Troy stretched out on the library rug in front of the blazing fire. Several games of checkers later, Troy yawned.

"Time for bed, young karateka."

"I'm not sleepy," he mumbled, his eyelids drooping.

"Of course."

After she helped him pack the game away, he shuffled out the door and up the stairs to his bedroom. "I'll be up to read you a story."

By the time Stella went upstairs, he'd fallen asleep and after dropping a kiss on his cheek, she headed back downstairs. Barely nine-thirty, she strolled into the kitchen and feeling at a loss, made a cup of cocoa. She cradled the mug between her palms and raised it to her lips. Steam tickled her nose and she smelled chocolate flavor before tasting sweetness.

"Mmm, this is good," she murmured, wandering into the living room.

Grabbing the remote from the coffee table, she flicked on the television and curled up on the sofa, hoping for a frivolous comedy to distract her from her tangled thoughts ... her life—Stan, the boy, the marriage, the future.

Finally, savoring the last chocolate drop, she flicked off the television and turned to go. She froze in her tracks.

"Don't go." Stan blocked the doorway, his hushed words like a caress upon her skin.

Chapter 11

Stella gripped the mug in her clammy hands. *Not a good idea, girl.*

"Stay." His one word, a whispered demand.

She knew she'd be playing with fire if she did, yet, something in his eyes beckoned. A weary look perhaps, or the tired way he ran his hand through his silver-streaked hair.

Still she hesitated. "I'd better no—"

In two strides he reached her, swept the cup from her fingers, set it on the table, took her hand and pulled her down with him on the sofa.

Breathless seconds ticked by.

He seemed fascinated by her slender fingers in his palm.

"Wha-at do you want?" Stella asked on a gasp of air.

"This." Stan raised her fingertips to his lips and tenderly kissed each one. "And this." Pulling her against him, he lifted the golden curls off her nape and laid claim to the spot with his lips. Then, he angled his mouth back up along her cheek to her mouth. "And this." His feather-light breath tickled her lips before his mouth came down upon hers.

Stella knew she'd come to regret this interlude ... he was the enemy, even if she was married to him. Hadn't he brought her up here for his own mercenary reasons?

His mouth on hers was like magic ... soft, pliant, sensual.

Just for a few minutes she wanted to forget, wanted to feel him close—the touching, the caressing, the loving. Pretend everything was all right. She melted into him, giving him kiss for kiss.

Stan lifted her into his arms and with his mouth still fastened on hers, crossed the room and climbed the stairs. He kicked the bedroom door open and shut, laid her on the bed and stretched out beside her. While his lips inched across her cheek and down her chin to feast at the pulse point at her throat, his hands undressed her, his fingers sliding beneath the lacy bra cupping her breasts.

A groan burst from his mouth, and he nibbled the sensitive area around her ear. Stella arched closer, breathing her delight. In a fever, she pulled his shirt apart and pressed her hands across his muscled torso.

Hard. Strong. Heady ... sexy.

"I've wanted—" He slid his hand along her thigh,

stroking the silky softness. "You are so beautiful," he breathed into her mouth, exploring deeper with his tongue.

A combustible moment ignited.

Stella whimpered ... she didn't want to, but she had to. Wrenching her lips away from his, she sucked in a mouthful of air, her insides breaking. She wriggled from beneath him, fighting against every strained nerve prodding her to curve back into his embrace, his warmth, his sexuality. To touch him, to love him.

"What?" A muscle battered his jaw, his breathing jerky. He rolled away from her, his body tense, controlled.

She averted her eyes, unable to meet his probing query. "Let me go."

But his fueled gaze pinned her down, a silent command to answer.

"I won't be used a second time." She shoved bunches of her hair off her brow. "To satisfy your male lust."

"What the—"

"Go away, Rogers." Through a blur, she tried to stare him down, but when he wouldn't be, she snatched up her sweatshirt. "I-I don't want—"

"You could've fooled me, lady." Stan slid off the bed and grabbed his shirt, a twist to his mouth.

"Not this way," she murmured more to herself than to him. "Just to--"

The rest of her words got lodged in her throat, and

she blinked rapidly, damming the tears threatening to spill.

"What?" He shoved his arms into his shirt, drew in a sharp breath, his facial muscles taut.

"To scoop the coup on the custody issue." She slammed him with her words, anger having pushed them from her throat, the same time she slipped her arms into her sweatshirt.

"You knew that," he admitted. "But I—"

"Get out." Stella scrambled off the bed, her breasts rising and falling, her hands fisted.

Stan muttered an expletive, the navy flecks in his eyes hardening. Without another word, he swept up a blanket and stomped from the room.

Stella collapsed to the floor and laid her head on the edge of the bed. For a long time she sat there, numb. Her eyes stung, her throat itched and her head throbbed. Things were going from bad to worse between them. She wanted to scream but only a croaking sound cracked from her lips.

Slowly, she pushed herself off the floor and stumbled to the bathroom. She splashed water on her face and it trickled down her neck, soaking her bosom. A hysterical sound bubbled from deep inside her. "Replay."

Stella trudged back and fell into bed, moonlight streaming across the covers, soothing. Thoughts jack-knifed through her mind. She tossed and turned. When she heard a footstep outside her door, she tensed, held her breath and waited for Stan to return.

He didn't.

The night seemed endless.

She squinted at the fluorescent hands of the clock. Four-thirty a.m. She groaned and pulled the blankets over her head. In another couple of hours, the household would be stirring awake. She had to get some sleep or she'd look the wreck she felt. Curled up and clinging to the covers all night, her muscles had stiffened. She stretched beneath the sheet and shivered as air circulated around her legs.

At that moment, she heard Stan walk into the room and froze, pretending to be asleep. She needn't have worried.

Within minutes, he'd showered, dressed and marched for the door. But was that a subtle pause by the bed? She pressed her fist to her mouth, squashing the temptation to peek at him.

Where had he slept, and where was he going at the crack of dawn?

Questions hammered her brain, but the answers floated in cyberspace.

That incident though, set the pattern for the following weeks. During the day, they kept their distance, speaking to each other only when necessary or when someone was nearby.

Had to keep up appearances.

Stella hated the pretense. But it was a waiting game until after the court hearing.

In the meantime, Joe or Fred drove her and Troy to the studio in Vancouver. The child joined her regular classes, manned the phone and helped with odd jobs. He tried so hard to please, and her heart went out to him. It would tear her apart when he was taken from her.

In the evening, one of the men chauffeured them back to the lodge.

During dinner, Troy took center stage by recounting his adventures in the dojo. His animated chatter kept them from having to feign conversation in front of him.

"Glad you're enjoying yourself, son," Stan said once, his voice warm, but his eyes on Stella chilled. "Not a nuisance, is he?"

"Of course not." Stella smiled at the child. "I love to have him."

After the meal, Stan worked out in the gym with Troy or went out for a trek in the woods. When he shut himself in his office, Stella took over spending time with Troy until he went to bed. Left on her own, she watched television, went for a swim or sat quietly reading a book. More often than not, the book slipped from her fingers and she sat alone, lost in her thoughts.

After everyone retired for the night, Stan collected

bedding and spent the night away from her. At the crack of dawn, before anyone woke up, he returned, piled the blankets in the closet, showered, dressed and departed.

Communication between them deteriorated to a brief nod and a curt goodnight. And tension stretched taut, ready to snap at the first provocation.

Stella lost weight. A touch of extra make-up hid the pallor of her face, but dark circles remained beneath her eyes, eclipsing her usual sparkle.

Stan had become grimmer, rarely smiling, his eyes hidden beneath his half-lowered lids. There were days when he appeared haggard, the gray above his temples more pronounced.

They were on the brink of disaster—living like intimate strangers.

Stella had caught Minni glancing at her with concern from time to time, but the older woman was wise enough to keep her counsel.

Life became a see-saw, up and down and all around. From the lodge, to the lawyers' office, to her studio and back to the mountain. The pace was grueling, seeming endless. A sigh burst from deep inside her. Even Christmas had caught them unaware, whizzing by without much ado. She'd been in town at her dojo. Stan and Troy at the lodge for the weekend when another snow blizzard raked the land, separating them on that magical day. Her sigh morphed into a moan but she muffled it behind her hand. Perhaps it had been an omen of what was to come.

Stella pressed her eyelids tight to stem the tears, the tension unbearable. Yet, feeling honor bound to uphold her end of the bargain, she could do nothing until Stan had custody of his son.

Their life ... their marriage was sitting on a time bomb.

And it was about to detonate.

* * *

Stan and Troy's mother had been deposed and the time had come for Stella to take the hot seat. While the world celebrated the start of the New Year, Stella prepped for a legal inquisition. The lawyers' interrogation challenged her quick wit, making her glad of her Martial Arts training to ward off any attack.

But, the legalities of the matter caused more delays. The mother persisted on fighting Stan for the child. Stan on the other hand, was determined to keep his son out of court.

As weeks slipped into months, the distance between them widened into a chilling chasm. But what would it matter?

After all this was a marriage deal, was it not?

It would soon be over ... her heart cracked.

At last, the day arrived for a face-off with the opposing party and their legal team. When the elevator panels slid open on the twenty-first floor of the towering downtown building, Stan cupped Stella's elbow and guided her toward the double doors at the end of the hallway. Suddenly, a woman in her mid-thirties, dressed in the height of fashion stormed by and bumped her shoulder. Stella stumbled. Stan grabbed her arm in a steely grip and kept her from falling, but the flush of embarrassment already suffused her face.

"Well-l, this must be the new momma," the woman drawled, feigning a French accent. She patted her jet-black hair in a perfunctory gesture, her eyes cold, hard. "The kid's mine," she spat. "Don't think your last-minute hook-up to this little ... er ... thing" —she glanced at Stella down her patronizing nose— "is going to change anything."

"Troy is not a possession, Ann." Stan stepped slightly forward, shielding Stella from the woman's venom. "You're his mother, but he will live with me, his father."

"We'll see who gets the kid." She turned a stiff back and laughing, glided through the huge office portals.

Chilled to the bone, Stella was glad of his protective arm about her shoulders.

Had to keep up appearances.

Sighing, she followed the echo of the woman's high-heeled shoes into the office with Stan.

186

Two hours later, Stella exited the office, her head buzzing with legal jargon and made a beeline for the water fountain by the elevators. Stan had remained behind to discuss details with his attorney. After taking a drink to soothe her parched throat, she glanced out the wide expanse of glass of one wall. The Vancouver skyline was overcast, the gray seas of Burrard Inlet choppy. Quite apropos, she thought, catching sight of a ferry sailing across to North Vancouver. She wished she were on it, far away from all this.

When she heard the door click open, Stella spun around and her eyes connected with Stan's for a fleeting moment. An uneasy feeling fluttered through her, and she clutched her purse between her damp palms. He rubbed his hand along his neck and walked across the hall, the grooves on his cheeks seeming to have deepened over the last two hours.

Stella wished she could hold him, say something to comfort him, but instead, she stayed where she was and queried him with her gaze.

"We're in for a fight."

"It's going to court?" Stella asked, her voice faltering.

"No." He took her elbow and ushered her into the elevator.

Once they reached the parking lot, he helped her into the Corvette; like the chopper, he rarely used it, but to navigate Vancouver traffic it was more practical than the Hummer or limo. He walked around, sliding into the driver's seat. "It's a sticky situation." He propped his hand on the steering wheel, tension vibrating from him, stifling in the confines of the cab. "Stella, I didn't know I had a son until a few months ago."

"What? Why? How?" The words tumbled from her mouth, and then she turned quiet, waiting. She had to know ... and he needed to tell her.

"When I was a college stud of twenty" –he broke off on seeing her elevated brows and pursed his lips, his gaze level with hers— "you must've been about seven at the time—"

"Eight." Her heart leaped. The same age as Troy now ... a child.

His lip tugged at the corner but didn't make it to a smile. He brushed his hand across his eyes and a gust of air blasted from his mouth. "On a foolish dare, I made the biggest blunder of my life—I married Ann."

A twitch of pain pierced her, until she remembered she'd been a child and he a man at the time.

"Within three months we split ... about nine years later she showed up on my doorstep, strung out and wanting to 'play house' ... we decided to give the marriage 'the ol' college try' again. I got smashed trying to get into the mood. By morning I had a doozer of a hangover but I knew without a doubt the big blooper had morphed into a mega mistake. I was about to voice my findings, but she'd already skipped town together with my cash and credit cards. The twenty-four hour 'reunion' ended in a speedy divorce, but with an unexpected prize ... a child I hadn't known existed for nine years."

Stella bit down the questions itching to spill off the tip of her tongue.

"There are no records to show I've given support for my son all these years." He pounded the steering wheel with his fist.

"But she accepted alimony?"

"Yeah."

"Well, that shows you wouldn't shirk your responsibilities."

A wan smile brushed his lips. "Gets tricky."

"And she's using it to her advantage."

"For all its worth." He inserted the key in the ignition, the half smile flipping to a hard line across his mouth.

"Why?" Stella clicked the buckle on her seatbelt. "I thought she didn't want the child on a regular basis."

"But she knows I do." He turned the key, revved the engine and steered the car into the stream of traffic on Burrard Street.

*   *   *

Stella settled against plumped-up pillows, drew the

blankets over her knees and tried to concentrate on a magazine. When she heard his footsteps outside the door, she held her breath and waited for him to come in, collect his bedding and leave as usual. Stan opened and shut the door, paused a loaded moment, and crossed the room with purpose.

Right to her.

"Wha-at are you doing?" she asked in barely a whisper, a tremor ripping through her.

"I'm getting into bed." His words firm, his gaze unflinching. "With my wife."

Chapter 12

Stella sat bolt upright. "You managed all right out of this bed for the last three months."

"Counting were you?" he said, a cocky grin on his mouth.

"You betcha," she let fly back. "Keeping tabs on my exit day."

"Fleet of foot and quick of mind." He chuckled, a dry sound. "Departure's not today."

"I thought you preferred to sleep elsewhe—"

"That was then. This is now." He cast her a cursory glance. "I'd turn that mag right side up if I were you."

Stella slammed the magazine on the nightstand, leaped off the bed and stood before him in her cotton nightie, her toes peeking beneath the frilly hem. "You can't."

"I can." He studied her from head to toe.

She blushed, crossed her arms over her breasts and curled her toes in the rug.

"I've no intention of sleeping out of a comfortable bed any longer."

He strode past her to the bathroom, tossing over his shoulder, "You're welcome to snooze on the library sofa ... a bit cramped though."

"Nothing has changed, Stan."

He spun around. "Honey, I've got so much shooting through my brain, all I want is a good night's sleep." He shut the door.

Cold air pierced her nightie, and Stella rubbed her arms to settle the goosebumps. She heard the shower running and reluctantly slid back into bed, her muscles coiling with tension. Propping a pillow against the headboard, she leaned back, bent her knees and pulled the covers to her chin.

A few minutes later, Stan walked from the bathroom, climbed into bed and turned off the bedside lamp. With a curt goodnight, he turned his back to her and in minutes he was sound asleep.

Stella released a pent-up breath, slid further under the blankets and closed her eyes, but sleep deserted her. After what seemed like hours, she slipped from the bed and paced the room. She rubbed her eyes and, pulling the curtain aside, glanced up at the star-studded sky, praying for an answer.

Thoughts tormented her mind.

She shared a house, bedroom and child with her

husband, but nothing more. Every pore in her body screamed with the frustration of living a lie.

As each day passed, she and Troy grew closer, yet she and her husband drew further apart. Stella knew what she had to ... must do. She pressed her fingers to her pounding temples, hoping she'd hold out until the conclusion of the custody battle.

She released the curtain and turned, staring at her sleeping husband. Moisture pressed against her eyelids and she blinked it away. She walked back to bed and quietly slid under the covers. A bedspring creaked and she twitched, her nerves strained to breaking point.

"Could we get some sleep, woman?" Stan's sleepy voice rippled across the stillness of the room.

He shifted to a more comfortable position and his leg brushed her thigh. Stella froze. When he made no other move toward her, she relaxed and soon after slept.

Another month dragged by.

One evening when Stella couldn't stand the charade any longer, she sat at her dressing table combing her hair. She took particular care with each stroke, sliding the comb through her curls, slow and easy. Otherwise, she might have pulled her hair out by the roots. When she neared the hundredth stroke, Stan walked in and plunked down on the edge of the bed.

"Game over."

The brush fell from her fingers, and she gaped at

him through the mirror.

"She consented. I have custody of my son."

Seeing the weary lines etched on his face, she swiveled around. "Thank, God."

"Copy that." He loosened his tie. "Thank you for all you've done."

Stella winced. He spoke to her like she was a stranger. She felt like her insides had been vacuumed out, leaving her empty, cold.

"What made her change her mind?" she asked, ignoring her racing heart. She had both dreaded and looked forward to this day.

Stan hauled himself up and tossed his tie over a hanger in the closet.

"Cash ... and more cash." He rubbed his thumb and index finger together in the age-old symbol for money. "A cush job overseas didn't hurt either."

"What?"

"Consultant for one of the couture houses in Paris." He unfastened the button at his shirt collar. "Jetting the globe with an entourage on shopping sprees and fashion shows suits her." He ran a hand across his eyes. "A small child would cramp her style."

"I see," Stella murmured, but she didn't really. Couldn't fathom how anyone could give up a beautiful child like Troy for a jet party. "Women can combine career and family and achieve success." She swallowed. "It isn't easy, but it can be done."

"Providing the woman is willing," he muttered. "Troy's mother isn't like that." A force of air burst from his mouth, and he scratched his bearded chin. "No doubt she loves him in her own way ... at least I'd like to think so. But she loves life in the fast lane more." He stripped the shirt off his back and hurled it in the laundry basket tucked in the corner of the closet. "She's made her choice, now she can live with it."

As I made mine, and must live with ... er ... without you. The thought flashed through her mind, and her pulse vaulted in her throat.

"Eventually, she'll realize what she's given up and want to see him."

As she was about to ... but she had no choice. The gulf between them stretched so wide, the boy could no longer keep them together.

"Could she?"

"Visitation rights were part of the agreement." Stan tightened his jaw. "Doubtful though, when she'll exercise them."

"How'd you think Troy would feel about that?" Stella hadn't moved from her spot by the dresser. She couldn't. Not wanting to break the delicate thread of confidence between them, she stared at her clasped hands in her lap, and waited for his answer.

This could be their last time together.

"He'll wonder about his mother and might wish to see her." He rolled his shoulders, working out the crick in his neck. "I won't stand in his way."

His words seemed to hold an underlying meaning for her too. She raised her eyes and sucked in her breath. He stood tall, every muscle of his chest defined, and gazed at her with such intensity she felt like he could read her mind ... her thoughts ... her heart. She wanted to run from him and yet at the same time run to him ... be enfolded in his arms. She wanted, needed, desired ... but she averted her gaze. It couldn't be as she wished, prayed for.

"Is Troy all right?"

"Yes." Stan unbuckled his belt. "He's resilient."

But he wasn't so sure he was.

Not with Stella looking so hot and sexy sitting on that chair.

The light from the lamp made her eyes luminous, turned her hair gold and revealed her curves beneath her nightgown. Her nipples strained against the fabric. His gut knotted. If he bent his head he could take one in his mouth, material and all. She shifted in the chair and the loose cotton slipped off her shoulder. If he snaked out his arm, he could pull her onto his lap, touch the velvet smoothness with his lips, lick with his tongue, nip ... Nestle his head upon her bosom, smell her scent, taste, touch her, needing her close, craving her softness, desiring ... her.

"I've spoken to Troy about his mother," he said, smothering the fantasy with the issue at hand. A deep sigh hurled from his mouth. "It's important for Troy to believe he's loved by both parents."

"How'd he take it?"

"Time will tell." He had his son back. And, wounds could heal ... he should know ... and he'd ensure no emotional scars remained on Troy's life.

"Why'd she fight you so hard then?"

"Financial gain was her aim. She pressured me for every penny she could get to keep the case out of court."

"She sold her child?" Stella blurted, her eyes widening in disbelief.

"And I bought?" Stan leaped from the chair, pacing the floor like a caged lion. "I suppose that's what it amounts to." He halted by her chair.

"Kinda like blackmail?"

Stan grunted. "Subtle, very subtle." He placed his hands on her shoulders, the contact electrifying, making her jump and him go into overdrive. "In addition to cashing out, she wanted a percentage of my domestic and global investments."

"Highway robbery."

He chuckled, albeit a dry sound, at her outrageous exclamation. "I offered her double the dough to keep her hands off my business."

"She accepted."

Stan nodded, holding her gaze, his thumb stroking the sensitive area along her neck. "She has what she wants and I have what I want ... well, almost." Her warmth, her feminine scent drifted to him, intoxicating, fueling his blood.

"You paid her and arranged for the job," Stella said, and it was more a recap of what he'd already said.

Stan winked, as if he'd been in control of the situation from the get-go. "I wanted her far away from Troy until he's old enough to decide whether he wants to see her or not."

"What'd the lawyers think about this arrangement."

"The financial agreement was drawn up privately between myself and Troy's mother. I gave her a post-dated check for half the money. When the custody papers are finalized, I'll pay her the rest."

His modus operandi was familiar. He'd done the same with her. Paid her to marry him ... and she'd accepted by cutting a high-end deal in her favor. Guilt gnawed at her insides. Was she any different? What did that make her? A mercenary gold-digger or a naïve fool? Especially since she had no intention of kee—

"As for the job," he shrugged, "she'll have to hold that on her own."

A telling silence pulsed between them.

"I'm glad you got what you wanted," Stella whispered.

"Just about."

Her head shot up. He wanted to get rid of her too. Desolation filled her. He wanted his freedom. Just him and his son like before. Breath jammed in her throat. Wasn't that what they'd agreed upon? What she wanted too? Her mind and her heart sparred, but her senses were attuned to his heat, the salt tang of his skin, his potent masculinity.

For a split second she closed her eyes, tilting back on the chair until it bumped the dresser, then she righted it. She lifted her lashes and clashed with his smoldering gaze. Her stomach flipped. Her pulse leaped.

"Stella, I-I," Stan said, his husky whisper an erotic caress upon her skin. He bunched her hair in his hands, cupping her face and lowered his head.

If he kissed her now, she'd be lost. She couldn't take that chance.

"Thi-is is as good a time as any to tell you."

He stopped a feather breadth from her lips. "Tell me what?"

Chapter 13

"I'm leaving."

"You're what?"

"I-I have to go." She turned away not wanting him to see tears brimming . "Please don't make it any harder than it already is."

"Case closed, you bolt." His lips twisted in a hard line. "Very well, go."

She blanched, his words like ice picks skewering her heart. He hadn't even tried to stop her. "I-I'd like to see Troy and explain."

"He loves you," he bit out, his eyes rivaling the Arctic tundra. "You'll break his heart."

"I've got to leave." Her lips trembled and a tear slid down her cheek. "Please, Stan, listen to me." Stella wiped the dampness off her face with the back of her hand. "I-I don't want to hurt him." Another tear fell and she swatted that too. "I-I love him—"

"Love?" He guffawed. "You're no better than the other one."

His words nearly crushed her. She swallowed the groan ready to erupt from her mouth and gripped the edge of the chair so hard her fingers hurt. A shaky breath, and she had her emotions under control, but her pulse pounded so fast she was sure she'd have a hole in her chest. "There's a way we can work this out."

"Apparently you've already done that." He grabbed a sweatshirt from the closet, pulled it over his head and yanked the door open. A pause in stride as if he wanted to say something more, then, without a backward glance, slammed it shut behind him.

The walls seemed to close around Stella. Blood pounded in her temples. She flung off her nightie, slipped into her jogging suit and sneakers and rushed downstairs. She grabbed a jacket from the foyer and fled to the sanctuary of the forest. The moonlit night was both a balm and a catalyst to her spirit. She had to leave. She collapsed against the trunk of a cedar, the bark rough beneath her palms. Her feelings for her husband were so overpowering, she'd go under if she didn't give herself some breathing space; to collect her thoughts, gain a new perspective on her life, her career, her future. Could it ever be with him, or would she travel the journey alone?

* * *

That night, Stella spent a lonely vigil on the library sofa. At dawn, she dragged her eyelids open and trudged up the stairs. She loathed to go into the bedroom but she squared her shoulders and hugging the bedclothes to her bosom, pushed the door open.

The bed was rumpled but Stan was nowhere about. Stella sighed with relief, tossed the blankets in the closet and made a beeline for the bathroom. In twenty minutes, she'd showered, changed and packed her bags.

After a hasty breakfast, she hugged Minni good-bye, bundled Troy in warm clothes and walked with him to the truck. Fred followed with their luggage and Minni kept pace beside him, clucking to Stella about her return.

"I don't know." Stella glimpsed concern in her eyes and avoided her gaze.

Troy skipped ahead and climbed onto the back seat of the Hummer. Stella curved her lips in a wistful smile, glad that to the boy this seemed like an adventure.

"Make it soon, Mrs." Minni glanced away, dabbing the corner of her eye with her apron.

Fred stashed the suitcases in the trunk and Joe slid onto the driver's seat, nodding in grim agreement.

Stella couldn't speak and forced a smile to her lips. Adjusting the strap of her shoulder bag, she glanced back at the lodge that had been her home for such a short but turbulent time. She swallowed her disappointment. He hadn't even come out to say good-bye. Blinking mistiness from her eyes, she took Fred's hand and he helped her climb onto the passenger seat.

*   *   *

Stan stood at the upstairs bedroom window and watched them drive off. His world was crashing around him and he didn't know if he could put it together. *So much for being in control.* Anger and disgust charged through him, but it was directed more at himself than at Stella. Had he made a wrong choice? Overplayed his hand with the woman? What other recourse had there been for him? He'd had no contingency plan. No plan B. No back up. His son's life had been at stake. He had to play his card. Had to play hard and win first time out. Even if it cost him all his net worth ... even if it cost him—

He smashed the windowsill with his fist and a growl ripped from him. Agony jabbed, and he tightened his abs. Had he won custody of his son, only to lose the woman he loved?

A guffaw stripped his throat raw.

There he'd admitted it, and it left a gouge in his gut.

An expletive tore from his mouth. Somehow she'd gotten under his skin ... well, he'd just have to get her out. One woman had made a fool out of him in his twenties; he wasn't about to have a repeat in his forties.

Could Stella also be holding out for more cash? One way to be sure. He'd wait it out.

*   *   *

Stella enrolled Troy at the school near her studio at English Bay. Due to the long drive between the lodge and the city, he spent the week with her and the weekend with his father. They hoped their separation appeared necessary, rather than intentional ... at least for the time being.

Although Troy spoke on the telephone with his father daily, Stan and Stella did not.

Weeks flew by.

Stella settled into her regular routine. Up at the crack of dawn for her daily run, Troy scampered beside her along the beach walk to the sound of seagulls. After a rushed breakfast, she'd get him off to school and work in the studio. She lacked the spark she had before but refused to dwell on the cause—one tall, blond and sexy husband.

Too troublesome.

After school, Troy bounded into the studio, grabbed a snack from the fridge and plopped in the chair by the desk. While she taught a class, he did his homework and answered the telephone until it was time for his own group lesson.

On a rare day when Stella had some free time, they bicycled around Stanley Park or rode the Sky Train. The child bloomed while she wilted as weeks rolled into months without a word from her husband.

When she waved Troy off for his weekend visit, she stood on the doorstep and watched the limo turn the corner, already missing him. To get through the two days, she worked longer hours, prepping for her next tournament, and once the last karateka left, stifling silence echoed the emptiness of her life.

To fill the void, she took in a movie or a meal with a girlfriend, or hopped on a bus to the Granville Island Market. Most often though, she walked along Robson Street—a cultural delight—sipping a bottle of water and on occasion indulged in a cup of coffee, the cool evening breeze helping to clear her mind.

On Sunday evening, Joe drove Troy back to the studio and always put a pie or cake in her hands from Minni. On this particular occasion, Troy leaped from the limo, his eyes bright with excitement.

"Guess what?"

Wind had ruffled his mop of dark hair and instead of wearing his jacket, he'd tied it around his waist. She bit her tongue on a reprimand and draped her arm around his shoulders, touching her lips to the top of his head.

"Dad's giving me a birthday party next weekend." He

slugged his fist in the air, and skipped ahead of her into the living room. "Yes!"

"Cool, that." She felt like she'd been blindsided with a front kick to the stomach, her heart throbbing.

What would happen when she and Stan divorced? Would he take Troy away from her? Would she ever be able to see him? The divorce would devastate her. Not seeing Troy would destroy her.

She closed the door and leaned her head on the jamb, breathing deeply.

"Would you teach my friends some Karate moves?" he called out.

"You trying to drum up more business?" Stella teased, straightening up.

Troy giggled and grabbed the remote control. "When I did my Kata, they looked at me kinda funny, until I explained I was practicing a fighting technique against an imaginary foe."

"You can invite them to the dojo anytime." Stella chuckled. "Now how about some popcorn, while we watch *The Challengers*?"

"Yeah!" Troy plopped down on the sofa, aimed the remote at the television screen and pressed the on button.

* * *

Next morning, Stella sat at her desk, picked up a marker and drew a red x over the date on the calendar. In three more weeks it would be one year since she landed on the ogre's doorstep floundering in the fishing net. A wistful smile tugged at her lips, but didn't make it to a full-fledged curve.

She rolled the pen between her thumb and forefinger. Living in limbo was not the answer. The time had come for a face-off with Stan to determine the course of their broken marriage.

The sudden ringing of the telephone shattered her contemplative mood. She picked up the receiver and froze.

Breathe.

She clutched the handle tighter, her heart tripping, her hands clammy, but thawed enough to say, "Troy's at the library with friends."

A long silence, then ... "Have him call me when he gets home," Stan commanded, his voice crackling through the line.

Home.

He called her place *home*. Did that mean something, or was it a slip of the tongue? In the next second, she got her answer.

With a curt good-bye, he hung up.

The dial tone echoed in her ear. She slammed the receiver down, tremors shaking her body, and for a long moment, she didn't move. Hurt turned to anger and pushing herself off the chair, she stomped onto the training floor, releasing her frustration on the heavy bag. Exhausted, she turned to leave and glimpsed her ashen face in the mirrored wall. She collapsed on the mat and buried her head in her hands. Up until then, she'd subconsciously been waiting for Stan to call, to say something, anything that would bridge the chasm between them.

Stella twisted her wedding band around her finger; for the umpteenth time she was tempted to tear it off her finger and hurl it against the wall. Still she couldn't do it. Her hand fluttered to her mouth, the cold metal of the ring a caress upon her lips. At the crossroads of indecision, despair swamped her and she gave free rein to the tears welling inside her.

She flicked wisps of hair off her forehead with the back of her hand and wiped her cheeks with her sleeve. She braced one hand against the mirrored wall and pushed herself up. Trudging off the training floor, she sank in the chair in the front office, propped her elbows on the desk, chin in her hands and thought of him up on his mountain retreat.

"Fine." She shoved her chair back with such force it tumbled to the floor. "He can stay there."

Shadows had crept into the room, and she flicked on the light switch. After she righted the chair, she marched into the kitchen, grabbed a pot and turned on the faucet full force. Troy would be home soon and he'd be hungry.

She shut the water off, slammed the pot on the stove, water splashing over the side and turned on the heat. A dash of salt dissolved in the water, and she reached up in the cupboard for a package of spaghetti and a can of tomato sauce. She pulled out strands of pasta and snapped them in half, all the while thinking of doing the self-same thing to—well, she wouldn't think of him. She tossed them in the boiling water, opened the can and dumped the contents in a smaller pan. A sprinkle of pungent oregano and basil followed, and she set the pan on the other heated element.

"Too bad, Mr. Arrogant Ogre." Stella plunged the wooden spoon in the sauce with a passion. "I make a mean spaghetti and you won't get a single bite." She stirred all the harder and a few droplets splashed out, sizzling on the stove.

The side door banged open and closed. "Who you talking to, Mom?" Troy skipped over to the table and reached for a piece of garlic bread, yet to be toasted.

"No one. And that bread isn't ready, yet." She slapped at his hand, missing.

"It's yummy, anyway." He grinned, munching on the piece he'd snatched.

"Don't talk with your mouth full. Now go wash up." She managed a smile but inside she was dying. "And call your father."

*　　*　　*

The day of Troy's birthday dawned bright and clear. It was September, the trees aflame with color, and a bonus in that rain had held off. Stella was jogging back to her studio when she stopped a moment to allow the beauty of the morning to seep into her soul. Surf crashed upon the shore, and a hazy veil hovered across the sky, muting the snow-capped mountains in the distance. It was on days like this that the sheer beauty of God's creation made her feel truly alive. She was a part of it and she was so very glad. She glanced up at a lingering star before sunlight chased it away. The last vestiges of night were fast disappearing and she breathed deeply, letting cool, morning air fill her lungs.

Stella picked up her pace, rounded her street corner, slowed to a trot, then a walk and stumbled to a stop. The side door of her studio was ajar.

Sure she'd locked it before she left, she frowned, alert. No one had a key except Troy and he'd left the previous afternoon for the lodge. It was six forty-five a.m. and Joe wasn't picking her up until ten-thirty.

Stella nudged the door open and with the stealth of a cougar, she slipped inside. The hallway was in shadow. A few more paces took her to her bedroom, and she peered inside; it was empty. Had she been so preoccupied about seeing Stan again, she'd forgotten to lock the door and merely pulled it shut? Could it have opened in the morning breeze?

The sound of footsteps echoed from the training floor.

Her heart battered her chest, and she swiped her damp palms on her thighs. In less than a split second, Stella spun around and with a silent tread, walked in that direction. Glimpsing a pair of black boots beneath the khaki colored drapes separating the gym from the office, she stopped. Hair on the back of her neck rose, and she sucked in a breath. Slowly, she let air ease between her clamped teeth and prepped for a possible attack.

"Who are you?" she called, a rush of adrenaline fueling her. "What're you doing in my studio?"

The intruder halted, mere inches from her on the other side of the curtain.

Chapter 14

A quiver shot through Stella, and she held her breath, gauging his next move.

The interloper closed a fist over a section of thick material, ready to shove it aside, but a sudden crash had him pull back. A cacophony of sound followed, mingling with his indecipherable words.

The thug was destroying her studio.

Stella focused on his boots, swung her leg beneath the folds, and with one sweep of her heel knocked him off his feet. Caught by surprise, he tumbled down, his breath heaving, his words muffled.

A split second before she burst through to confront him, he leaped up and lunged for the opening. A tense filled moment hurled past, the curtains the only barrier between them. Stella raised her right leg, pivoted and landed a sidekick to his chest. He fell backward and dragged the drapes, rods and all, down with him, his groan muted by the crash.

Her assailant lay sprawled on the floor amidst trophies and overturned chairs, trying to disentangle himself from the folds of the fabric. Stella reached out to lift the cover off him and he swung his legs, skimming her above the ankles. The speed and impact of his attack knocked her off balance, and she fell to the floor.

Confidence is good, over confidence can backfire.

Concealed by yards of cloth, he grabbed for her, but she rolled away, landing a double front kick to his abdomen. With a muffled oath, he staggered back and she shot up, securing a defensive stance. Just as quickly, he rebounded, coming within her range and she kiead aloud, smacking him with a spinning back kick to his chest. The thick material cushioned the blows, so she followed with a double forward punch to his jaw. He blocked the first, but she made contact with the second. He stumbled backward and growled under his camouflage, far from being knocked out.

She couldn't put a dent on this man.

It was time to call 911 and have the police take over. She didn't have time for this combat; she had a birthday party to attend. At this thought, a faint smile feathered her lips and she slid back another step. Within reach of the telephone, she turned to lift the receiver and he tossed the covering over her.

"Never, ever, turn your back on an opponent." The

cloth smothered her words and she tried to disentangle herself from it.

"You carry a powerful punch, Mrs. Rogers," the man said, encircling her with his arms.

"Oomph, let me go." Stella tried to twist away. His familiar scent and deep voice sent shivers of another sort up her spine and she swatted at him.

He shifted, holding her with one arm while he swept the fabric off her with the other. The moment she tossed her head back, her eyes sparred with his—violet-blue flame versus cobalt ice.

"You—you ..." she sputtered, struggling to get out of his arms. His aftershave wafted to her, his body heat melting her and his breath tickled her nape. "What're you doing here?"

"You left this behind." He pulled an envelope from his jeans' pocket. "Tsk, tsk, careless of you." He wedged the envelope in her cleavage, his fingers brushing her skin.

She sucked in a breath.

He jerked at the contact, her sizzle spearing him to the core.

"I don't want—"

"A deal's a deal." He winked.

She struggled to shake him off. Couldn't do it.

"I would've delivered it earlier," he said. "But I figured you'd come to your senses—"

"Me?"

"—and return to claim it yourself." He shrugged his indifference, but the throbbing of his pulse at his temple cued that he was anything but. He tightened his jaw. A nuisance. The feeling of falling into her persisted. So, he went on the offensive. "Time to come clean, set the record straight."

"What do you mean?"

"You walked away from a mil, you might be holding out for more—"

"No!"

"That's mighty confusing." He scratched his head with his knuckles.

"If you don't want the mil, maybe you're wanting something" –he mocked a cough—"someone?"

Me, he thought, his gut clenching at the possibility. He'd waited nine months ... nine long dry months while he got his pride in order. When she didn't come for her 'pay' and didn't demand more cash, he dared to believe again in the real deal. Then, he'd called, heard her voice and that sealed the merger.

Stella shook her head. "I—I don't—"

"Let's find out shall we?" He flashed her his sexiest grin. "A lot's at stake here" –his eyes zeroed in on her breasts, skimmed over the envelope nestled there and focused on her nipples pushing against the fabric of her gui—"and it has very little to do with dollars and cents."

She inhaled sharply and stepped back, but his arms were like a steel band around her. And he liked that just fine. His grin turned wolfish. "What now, Sensei?"

"Let me go," Stella demanded, every nerve in her body vibrating with awareness. "You're acting like an ape-man—"

"If you say so." And with that, he threw her over his shoulder, curtain and all and stalked through the studio until he sighted the bedroom. A lazy smile curved his mouth. He kicked the door open, marched inside and tossed her on the bed.

"Don't." She swallowed, willing her churning emotions to subside. "Not like this."

"How would you like it then, Mrs. Rogers?" he asked, voice husky.

Chapter 15

Stan followed, his weight pressing the mattress down and holding her captive amidst the pillows. His eyes shadowed, and he bent his head, claiming her lips.

Stella lowered her lashes, her pulse racing and her stomach fluttering. His mouth could create magic over her body ... she craved ... wanted ... until she remembered nine months of angst.

This was easy, just too easy.

Wouldn't do to capitulate and fall like a ripe peach smack in his palm, even if every nerve in her body vibrated with wanting him.

Stella yanked his hair, hard.

"What the..." With a muffled oath, he pulled her hands away and held them above her head.

"I'm so-o mad at you." She glared at him and her heart jerked out of rhythm, the taste of him still upon her lips.

"Can you ... uh ... be mad at me, later?" he murmured,

trying to check her squirming beneath him. "That's not helping." He rolled over and dragged her on top of him, his arousal evident.

It stirred her blood with desire, her heart with longing. Dear God, she really loved him, this man who had caused her such heartache. She shut her eyes tight, rising passion banishing tormenting memories. Reveling in the scent and feel of him, she wanted to wrap her limbs around his, holding him close, and succumb to his sexual magnetism. She inhaled a gust of oxygen, exhaled and punched him in the stomach instead.

"Enough," he growled, reaching for her hand.

She managed to twist away, scrambling off the bed and vaulting for the Ninja sword on the opposite wall. "This is how I'd like it, Mr. Rogers."

Swishing the blade through the air, she advanced on him.

"Watch it, Stella."

"Absolutely." She browsed his body, strong and sinewy and mobile. A quiver shot through her, and her heart hurled against her ribs. "Strip."

He hesitated.

"Stand up."

He narrowed his gaze, a storm brewing beneath his lashes, and he shuffled off the bed, towering above her.

"Unbutton your shirt."

"You want a war, Stella?"

She shook her head. "A battle will do."

"Yes, ma'am." He inserted his fingers in the top button and worked his way down.

"Slow 'n easy."

"Don't like my method?" He cocked a brow. "You do it."

"No." She caught her bottom lip between her teeth.

A muscle ticked at his jaw.

Seconds later, his shirt hung open, sunlight curls across his chest beckoned. Her fingers itched to touch, her mouth to—she averted her gaze, stumbled onto his sex, then bounced up, falling into the ocean of his eyes. Her stomach took a dive, her breath jamming in her throat. "Shed it."

At a lazy pace, he slid the shirt off his shoulders and it fell in a pile of white cotton at his feet.

"Now ... uh—" She cleared her throat. "Your belt."

He dropped his hand to the buckle, his smoldering gaze drilling into her. When he moved his fingers—she held her breath the belt hung loose she exhaled in a rush.

"Undo the snap." Her heart somersaulted.

She'd just lit the fuse to the powder keg.

He narrowed his gaze to blue slits, cooperating.

"Zipper."

As slow as molasses, he slid the zipper down, jeans gaping at the front, his solid length straining for release through the thin material of his briefs. She swallowed around the constriction in her throat, heat zapping into her body and sending her pulse skyrocketing. She wanted ... it had been so long ... but she couldn't have him ... not yet ... not until—

"What now?"

"I ... uh ... I—" She stopped, rallying her thoughts to the forefront. "Shoes, socks off."

"Sure thing," he said, his tone flippant. He bent down, removed one shoe, then the other, and before she blinked, tossed a black sock in her face.

"Wha-a-t?" Stella swayed backward.

"Power shift." He knocked the blade from her hand and twirled the handle around his fingers. "Nice."

"We'll see," she murmured, calculating his next move.

He advanced.

She retreated.

He took another step and pointed the gleaming tip at her cleavage.

"Wha-at 're you going to do?" She wiped her moist palms on her silk-clad thighs, wishing she hadn't given in to the perverse urge to wear *his* gui to jog in.

"Finish the job you started." A wicked grin played on his lips. "You'll do the honors."

She took two paces back. "No."

He took two steps forward. "Yes."

"I-uh—" She slid her tongue across her bottom lip.

"Stop that," he muttered, tweaking his golden earring with his thumb and forefinger.

He looked like a pirate.

A hot and sexy buccaneer.

She swallowed. "I-I don't think—"

"Be still, woman."

She stopped moving.

He placed the blade at the gaping 'V' of her top, and flipping it to one side exposed the swell of her breasts.

She stopped breathing.

Stan slid the point down the front of her Karate gui, slicing the sash at her waist in half. In a hush, red silk slithered to the floor, coiling at her feet.

A shallow puff of air burst from her lungs.

The silk parted, revealing a vista of such feminine beauty, a tremor shook him, desire fueling him. Her breasts were veiled by sheerest white lace, her nipples straining to be free. "You take my breath away."

Air sounded between his teeth and a muscle throbbed along his jaw. He reached for her. He pulled back. Not yet. He frowned, planning his next move, and a smile lifted the corner of his mouth.

"Aha!'

Her eyes flew open.

With a flick of his fingers, he slit the tie holding up her pants. Soft material shimmied down her legs and pooled at her feet.

"Step out of them."

She hesitated.

"Now, please."

She arched a shapely brow and did as he requested. "Now what?" Her chin shot up a notch.

"Let me think." He scratched his head with the hilt, watching her through half-shuttered eyes. The two scraps of lace covering her breasts and dusky curls between her hips, tantalized ... he wanted to touch, feel, taste. An inferno blazed inside him, and he raised a hand, blotting sweat beading his forehead. She should be showing some vulnerability, but instead, she stood in the middle of the floor like a champ.

"I want you lying on the bed, woman." He stepped behind her, prompting her forward with the metallic point.

"I don't think so." She stayed her ground.

"How so?"

"You heard me," she said, her voice a seductive whisper. "You want me on the bed, you'll have to get me there."

"And when I do?" He twisted a loose curl from her ponytail around his index finger.

"If—"

He laughed. "A challenge any man worth his salt—"

"And you're not any man." Her words soft as the silk that had draped her body, fell over him like a caress.

222

"That's right."

She smiled, pleased.

He caught that from the corner of his eye and scowled. Of course, he knew what she was up to. If he let his guard down, even for a second, she'd have him flipped on his back. She was a lightweight, but she knew self-defense—a real pro. "Yep."

When he didn't move, she took a step away from him towards the door. And another.

"Stop."

"No."

"Yes."

She froze in her tracks, the kiss of steel smack center on the clasp of her bra. With a practiced touch, he opened the catch, exposing the smooth expanse of her back. He edged closer, his hips brushing her buttocks.

She drew in a sharp breath.

He skimmed the straps of lace from her shoulders and nuzzled her nape. She sighed, ruffling combustible air around them. His hands glided along her back, moved around her midriff and upward until her breasts filled his palms. The sword dipped from his fingers.

"Unfair advantage," she whispered, arching into him.

"All's fair in ..." He eased her around and took her lips in a hot kiss. His tongue slid into her mouth, teasing, tasting, dueling with hers.

He pulled her smack against his steel shaft, her

breasts pressed against his chest, his hands cupping her buttocks. He rocked with her to the tempo of the mating waltz in her mouth. The sword dropped from his busy fingers onto the carpet. She made a slight movement.

"Uh uh," he breathed into her mouth and scooped her up in his arms.

Without breaking the kiss, he strode to the bed and lowered her upon it. He reclined beside her, the mattress springs creaking beneath his weight, his thumb brushing the pulse point at the base of her throat. "You are so beautiful." He dipped his mouth to her heartbeat, licking. Then, he traveled lower and buried his face in her bosom, sweet musk assailing his nostrils. "Woman, what you do to me."

Settling his mouth over her breast, Stan stroked with his tongue, his teeth nipping the hard bud ... ecstasy. His thumb tweaked her other nipple to erection, then, he slid his fingers down her midriff, dallied at her navel and explored lower. He stripped the scrap of lace from her hips and slipped his fingers inside her moist folds, fondling.

"Stan," Stella gasped, arching into him. She spread her hands across the muscles of his back, then upward to his nape, her fingers frolicking in frenzy through his hair.

Stan sought every sweet inch of her with his hands, his body, his mouth. He was on fire and in seconds, he shed the rest of his clothes. He rained kisses everywhere on her body. His tongue ignited a trail of moist heat toward her navel, paused to taste, and explored lower, burying his face in her warm nest of curls. Dear heaven, how had he lived without her all these months. He hadn't, of course. He'd merely been existing.

"Stella ..."

"Yes."

Blood pulsed through him, he was rock hard, his breathing heavy. He took his weight on his elbows, exerting a check on his unbridled passion, then plunged deep inside her slick folds. He thrust into her again and again, drinking in her moan of pleasure with his mouth. Like wildfire out of control, he rode her fast and deep and high, holding onto her, not wanting to lose her on the climb. He gasped for air, thinking he'd die soaring with her to the pinnacle. A suspended stillness when passion spiraled in a tight coil, then Stella shattered, pulsing beneath him ... he exploded.

"You're mine," he panted, brushing his lips across her moist brow.

"Yes." She placed a chaste kiss on his cheek, a seductive smile curving her lips. "And you're mine." She smoothed her hands across his chest, stroked his nipples, then licked each one with the tip of her tongue.

He groaned, a guttural sound from deep in his throat. She explored further down his muscled torso, brushing her fingers over the bullet of hair shooting to his navel and further. Pausing, she dipped her fingertip inside the crevice, then journeyed lower, skimming his hard length with her hand. She lifted a finger to her mouth, licked, and stroked his surging erection with the moist tip.

"Dear God, Stella." He held her hand to the spot.

"Mmm, husband?"

"You want to kill me?"

"Just a little bit ... with love."

He nodded, resigned. "Proceed, wife."

*   *   *

Two hours later, Stan helped Stella from the Hummer and hand in hand they walked to the lodge.

"Oh, hi!" Troy bounded out the door and flung himself at them.

"Didna I tell ye, lad, not to leave without a coat," Minni clucked after him, wiping her hands on her apron and shaking her head.

"We're coming in, Minni." Stan tossed his son over his shoulder and stomped into the house, Stella by his side.

Later that night, after Troy had gone to bed, Stan plunked down on the library sofa and pulled Stella onto his lap. "It's been a full house for our karateka."

He pressed a kiss on the crown of her head.

"And a full heart ... like Christmas," she murmured the last words beneath her breath, but he heard.

He tilted her chin with his knuckle and gazed deep into her eyes. "We will make everyday like Christmas, my love." Then, he chuckled. "Troy will definitely vote for that."

Stella smiled and wrapped her arms around his neck, tenderness tugging at her heartstrings. "He 'll be up at the crack of dawn."

"Yeah." Stan flashed her his sexiest smile, and breath caught in her throat. He scooped her up in his arms and strode out and up the stairs to their bedroom. A suspended moment ... a heartbeat ... and, he lowered his head, his mouth a feather-breadth from her own. "But tonight is ours, Mrs. Rogers ... and tomorrow ... and forever."

Also by Sun Chara

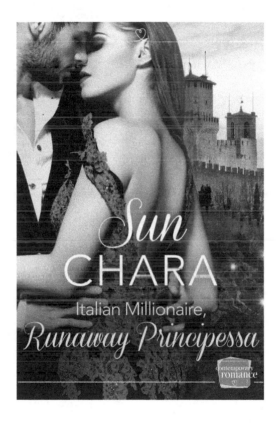

Italian Millionaire, Runaway Principessa

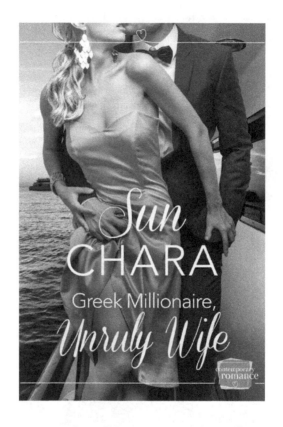

Greek Millionaire, Unruly Wife

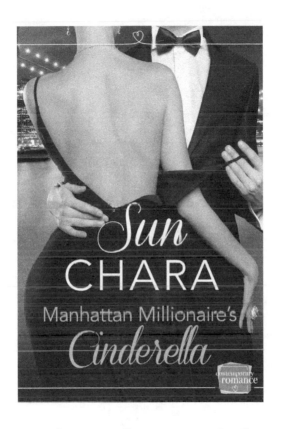

Manhattan Millionaire's Cinderella

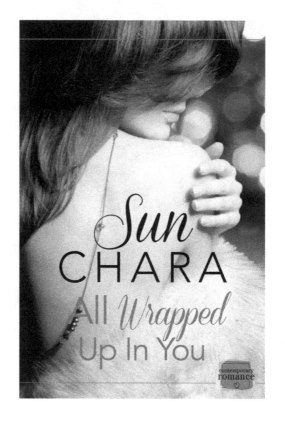

All Wrapped Up in You